Rafiq's dark gaze swept over Kiley, settling on her face. "You're very beautiful," he said.

"Thank you."

"Do you believe me?"

"I want to."

"You should believe." He took a step closer. There was something about his eyes, something…

"What are you thinking?" she asked, half-afraid of the answer.

"That I want you. I will not have you. Not yet, but I want you."

His words made her tremble as an emotion swept through her—one she couldn't identify right away. And then she knew.

Desire.

Dear Reader,

If you're eagerly anticipating holiday gifts we can start you off on the right foot, with six compelling reads by authors established and new. Consider it a somewhat early Christmas, Chanukah or Kwanzaa present!

The gifting begins with another in *USA TODAY* bestselling author Susan Mallery's DESERT ROGUES series. In *The Sheik and the Virgin Secretary* a spurned assistant decides the only way to get over a soured romance is to start a new one—with her prince of a boss (literally). Crystal Green offers the last installment of MOST LIKELY TO... with *Past Imperfect,* in which we finally learn the identity of the secret benefactor—as well as Rachel James's parentage. Could the two be linked? In *Under the Mistletoe,* Kristin Hardy's next HOLIDAY HEARTS offering, a by-the-book numbers cruncher is determined to liquidate a grand New England hotel...until she meets the handsome hotel manager determined to restore it to its glory days—and capture her heart in the process! Don't miss *Her Special Charm,* next up in Marie Ferrarella's miniseries THE CAMEO. This time the finder of the necklace is a gruff New York police detective—surely he can't be destined to find love with its Southern belle of an owner, can he? In *Diary of a Domestic Goddess* by Elizabeth Harbison, a woman who is close to losing her job, her dream house and her livelihood finds she might be able to keep all three—*if* she can get close to her hotshot new boss who's annoyingly irresistible. And please welcome brand-new author Loralee Lillibridge—her debut book, *Accidental Hero,* features a bad boy come home, this time with scars, an apology—and a determination to win back the woman he left behind!

So celebrate! We wish all the best of everything this holiday season and in the New Year to come.

Happy reading,

Gail Chasan
Senior Editor

Please address questions and book requests to:
Silhouette Reader Service
U.S.: 3010 Walden Ave., P.O. Box 1325, Buffalo, NY 14269
Canadian: P.O. Box 609, Fort Erie, Ont. L2A 5X3

SUSAN MALLERY

THE SHEIK AND *THE* VIRGIN SECRETARY

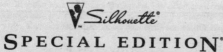

SPECIAL EDITION

Published by Silhouette Books

America's Publisher of Contemporary Romance

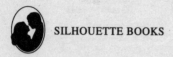

SILHOUETTE BOOKS

ISBN 0-373-24723-0

THE SHEIK AND THE VIRGIN SECRETARY

Copyright © 2005 by Susan Macias Redmond

This edition published by arrangement with Harlequin Books S.A.

® and TM are trademarks of Harlequin Books S.A., used under license.
Trademarks indicated with ® are registered in the United States Patent
and Trademark Office, the Canadian Trade Marks Office and in other
countries.

Visit Silhouette Books at www.eHarlequin.com

Printed in U.S.A.

Books by Susan Mallery

Silhouette Special Edition

Tender Loving Care #717
More than Friends #802
A Dad for Billie #834
Cowboy Daddy #898
*The Best Bride #933
*Marriage on Demand #939
*Father in Training #969
The Bodyguard & Ms. Jones #1008
*Part-Time Wife #1027
Full-Time Father #1042
*Holly and Mistletoe #1071
*Husband by the Hour #1099
†The Girl of His Dreams #1118
†The Secret Wife #1123
†The Mysterious Stranger #1130
The Wedding Ring Promise #1190
Prince Charming, M.D. #1209
The Millionaire Bachelor #1220
‡Dream Bride #1231
‡Dream Groom #1244
Beth and the Bachelor #1263
Surprise Delivery #1273
A Royal Baby on the Way #1281
A Montana Mavericks Christmas:
  "Married in Whitehorn" #1286
Their Little Princess #1298
**The Sheik's Kidnapped Bride #1316
**The Sheik's Arranged Marriage #1324
**The Sheik's Secret Bride #1331
‡‡The Rancher Next Door #1358
‡‡Unexpectedly Expecting! #1370
‡‡Wife in Disguise #1383
Shelter in a Soldier's Arms #1400
**The Sheik and the Runaway
  Princess #1430
Christmas in Whitehorn #1435
**The Sheik & the Virgin Princess #1453
**The Prince & the Pregnant Princess #1473
*Good Husband Material #1501
The Summer House:
  "Marrying Mandy" #1510
*Completely Smitten #1520
*One in a Million #1543
*Quinn's Woman #1557
A Little Bit Pregnant #1573
Expecting! #1585
**The Sheik & the Princess in Waiting #1606
**The Sheik & the Princess Bride #1647
**The Sheik & the Bride Who Said No #1666
**The Sheik and the Virgin Secretary #1723

Silhouette Intimate Moments

Tempting Faith #554
The Only Way Out #646
Surrender in Silk #770
Cinderella for a Night #1029
Living on the Edge #1383

Silhouette Books

36 Hours
The Rancher and the Runaway Bride

Montana Mavericks Weddings
  "Cowgirl Bride"

World's Most Eligible Bachelors
Lone Star Millionaire

Sheiks of Summer
  "The Sheik's Virgin"

Harlequin Books

Montana Mavericks: Big Sky Grooms
  "Spirit of the Wolf"

Harlequin NEXT

There's Always Plan B #1

Harlequin Historicals

Justin's Bride #270
Wild West Wife #419
Shotgun Grooms #575
  "Lucas's Convenient Bride"

*Hometown Heartbreakers
†Triple Trouble
‡Brides of Bradley House
**Desert Rogues
‡‡Lone Star Canyon

SUSAN MALLERY

is the bestselling and award-winning author of over fifty books for Harlequin and Silhouette Books. She makes her home in the Los Angeles area with her handsome prince of a husband and her two adorable-but-not-bright cats.

Chapter One

"I wondered if you were currently looking for a mistress," Kiley Hendrick said quietly.

Prince Rafiq of Lucia-Serrat stared at the woman sitting across from him. He had thought the biggest surprise of his Monday had been to find Kiley at her desk that morning, instead of on her honeymoon.

He had been wrong.

"You speak of yourself?" he asked.

She nodded, keeping her gaze firmly on the pad of paper she clutched on her lap.

He hadn't seen his secretary in five days. She'd taken off part of the previous week to prepare for her impending marriage. "I take it the wedding on Saturday was not a success," he said.

"There was no wedding." She raised her head and stared directly at him. "Eric and I are no longer together."

"I see."

He allowed his gaze to return to her tightly clenched hands and saw that the modest diamond engagement ring was no longer on her left hand. A thin indentation on her pale skin was the only proof it had existed at all.

"I know that you are currently between, ah, women," she said and blushed. "That is, I sent the final gifts and letter so I thought that you had broken up." She pressed her lips together as if not sure how to continue.

"I am no longer seeing Carmen," he offered helpfully.

Kiley nodded. "Yes. I thought so. And while I know you usually have one or two candidates waiting in the wings, I wondered if you would consider me. Even though I'm not your usual type."

He had a type? "Meaning?"

She released her death grip on her pad of paper and shifted in her seat. "Glamorous. Beautiful. Sophisticated. I'm okay looking, but not in their league. But you've only seen me in work clothes. I clean up pretty well. I'm smart, I have a sense of humor." She paused and bit her lower lip. "I've never had a conversation like this. I don't know what you're looking for when you pick a woman for, um, well, that."

"My bed?"

The blush returned. She swallowed but didn't look away. "Right. Your bed."

Rafiq had not discussed things so openly before, either. He leaned back in his chair and considered what he looked for in a mistress.

"Obviously some physical beauty," he said, more to

himself than her. "But that is less important than one might think. Intelligence and humor are required. Not every waking moment is spent making love. There is plenty of time for conversation."

He thought of Carmen's shrill demands. "An even temper would be desirable."

"You've known me for two years," Kiley reminded him. "I've never gotten angry."

"Agreed." She had not. She was efficient, organized and very much responsible for the ease with which his workday progressed. But his mistress?

While Kiley was attractive and he would admit to finding pleasure in watching her move, he had never considered that more than a bonus. Beautiful, sensual women were easy to find. An excellent assistant was not.

The most sensible course was to politely thank her for the offer, then refuse the invitation. He would—

"There will be advantages," she said, as if trying to convince him. "I understand your work. We can discuss it, if you'd like. Plus I won't mind if you have to stay at the office late."

"Most likely you will be working late with me," he said, wondering why this was so important to her. What had pushed the normally reserved Kiley to make such an outrageous—for her, at least—request?

"Yes, there is that." She cleared her throat. "I don't know what else to say. I just hope you'll consider me."

He had never been approached so openly by a woman intent on joining him in his bed. He would have bet a considerable part of his fortune that she was not the type to be interested in an affair. He still believed that.

"Why do you want to do this?" he asked.

Kiley returned her attention to him. Her dark-blue eyes flashed with pain. "Revenge."

"A noble motive. I assume this revenge is because of your fiancé?"

"Yes. Eric."

She paused, as if considering how much to tell him. Rafiq could guess the basic scenario, but he wanted to hear it from her. He wanted to gauge her emotions and her intent.

While she chose her words, he looked at her. Really looked—not at the ever-present secretary who antici-pated his needs and made his life flow pleasantly, but at the woman.

She was of average height—perhaps five foot four or five inches. Her hair, worn short and layered, was the color of gold. Or perhaps the north-shore beaches of Lu-cia-Serrat at sunset. Her large eyes dominated her face. He'd noticed how the deep blue darkened or lightened with her mood. He had always been able to tell if she was annoyed with him.

She was delicately built, small-boned, with curves that intrigued him. Now he took in the slight swell of her breasts and the shape of her calves below the hem of her knee-length skirt.

She was attractive, he thought. He found her easy to be with. She did not scream or annoy him. Like every other woman of his acquaintance, she wanted something from him. Unlike the others, she had been honest from the first.

But did he want her in his bed?

"He cheated," Kiley said at last, obviously fighting tears. "I'm sure you guessed that. He spared me the cli-

ché of the groom sleeping with the bride's maid-of-
honor-slash-best friend, but he more than made up for
it in other ways. He had sex with most of the women in
his law school class, his neighbors, my neighbor, along
with countless others. He propositioned two of my
friends. At the time, they tried to tell me, but I wouldn't
listen. Talk about stupid."

She spoke lightly, as if the words had no meaning.
But he heard the pain in her voice and saw it in her eyes.

"You did not believe them?" he asked.

She shook her head. "I was fooled right up until last
Friday morning when I walked in on him and a woman
from his study group." She blinked rapidly as if holding in tears. "That wasn't even the worst of it. He c-came
after me and told me it didn't mean anything." She
paused to swallow, the tears closer to the surface now.
"He never was very original. Then he told me that he
was doing it *for* me. That he wanted to treat me with reverence and respect. So he kept that side of himself away
from me."

She looked at Rafiq. "My idea of loving someone, of
feeling reverence, isn't to cheat on her over and over
again."

"You canceled the wedding." If Rafiq had planned to
attend, he would have known before now. But an out-
of-town commitment had caused him to send his regrets.

"Eric was shocked, if you can believe it," Kiley said.
"He actually thought I'd still go through with it because
it was the next day and we had 250 people coming. Everything was paid for. But I wouldn't do it. I loved him and
I thought he loved me and I was wrong. Getting married
at that point would only make things worse. So I canceled."

She dropped her head and stared at the pad of paper on her lap. "My mom and I made phone calls. We couldn't get everyone, so I went to the church the next morning and told them as they arrived." She took a deep breath. "It was horrible."

"You? Not Eric?"

She shook her head. "He took the tickets for our honeymoon in Hawaii and left with his flavor of the week. I hope they get rashes. And stung by jellyfish."

Her courage surprised him. She could easily have sent a family member to stand at the church, but she'd done it herself.

"Why me?" he asked.

For the first time since walking into his office, a smile tugged at her lips. "You're a prince, Rafiq. That makes you the best candidate around."

"Ah. I see." He could discern out the rest of it. "Eric has accepted a job with the law firm I use. Therefore he will attend some of the same functions I do. As my mistress, you would go with me."

"Exactly. Eric doesn't like you," she added. "I think he's jealous. He's tried to get me to quit a few times, but I refused. He would talk about the women in your life as if they were sluts or something but I'm starting to believe he was envious. He wants what you have. Or maybe he wants to be you. I don't know and I don't care. But I'm convinced that my being your mistress will destroy him."

Rafiq considered her words. He had only met Kiley's fiancé one or two times. He'd never formed an opinion of the man until now.

"Do you want him destroyed?" he asked.

She nodded. "Then I want to walk away and forget he ever existed." She looked at him. "There's another reason I came to you. You're a good man. You'd never treat a woman the way Eric treated me. You'd simply end things without any of the lies."

Her assessment of his character was interesting. He could name twenty people who would do their best to convince her he was the biggest bastard on the planet. But she was also right—he'd never lied to a woman. He'd never stooped to trickery or deception.

Was he considering her offer? Did he want Kiley as his mistress? He wouldn't mind her in his bed, despite the complications. He liked her. The proposition had possibilities.

"There are logistics to be considered," he said. "If we decide to move forward with this."

They were discussing things so calmly, Kiley thought, more than a little amazed by the turn of events. She was willing to admit she was still emotionally numb from the shock of Eric's betrayal, but even as she'd imagined a thousand ways this conversation could go, she'd never thought it would be so rational. Maybe this sort of thing happened to Rafiq all the time, but it was a definite first for her. Still, she was determined. She could forgive a lot of things, but not betrayal on that level. Not ever.

To think that Eric had tried to make her feel guilty about enjoying her job with Rafiq when Eric had been cheating on *her.* She'd been so careful not to talk about her boss and she'd always gone out of her way to reassure Eric. Just the thought of it made her want to throw something.

He had even complained about Rafiq's generous gift of Baccarat crystal. A gift she currently had boxed up in her office to return to her boss.

"You're the expert," she told him. "You're going to have to come up with the list."

He smiled. "Of course. First there is the matter of what the relationship would entail."

Okay, this might be the first time she'd ever applied to be a mistress, but she was fairly sure the ground rules were simple.

"I thought it would be about sex," she said, then wished she hadn't as his dark eyebrows rose slightly.

"Sexual accessibility is assumed," he told her. "You would be as available as I wished and vice versa."

He would be available to her? Interesting thought. Not that she could imagine herself picking up the phone and telling him to get naked and get ready.

"There is also the matter of fidelity," he continued. "During our time together, there are to be no other men in your life and no other women in mine."

"That one's easy," she said. "I'm not the unfaithful type."

"Consider carefully," Rafiq said. "The human heart is a contrary organ. Your goal is to punish Eric and make him jealous. During the course of our affair, he could try to win you back. By the terms of this agreement, that would not be allowed."

"You don't have to worry about that. There is nothing Eric can ever say or do to make me think of him as anything but a lying worm."

Rafiq didn't look convinced. Kiley knew it didn't matter what he thought. Eric was *her* problem. She could still feel the disbelief that had flooded her when she'd walked into his apartment. He'd given her the key several weeks ago but she'd never used it. Somehow it hadn't felt right. But on the day before their marriage, she'd decided to pay him an unexpected visit and take him breakfast. Only, she had been the one to get the surprise.

She was still in shock. It had been three days, and the truth of what had happened had barely begun to sink in. Part of her was glad. She wasn't looking forward to the moment when the pain hit full force.

"There is also the matter of us working together," Rafiq said. "You are too efficient for me to let go."

"That's fine. I want to keep working. I need to pay my parents back for all the money they spent on the wedding. I have most of it already. You pay me very well and I've been saving so Eric and I could have a down payment for a house. This is Los Angeles and real estate is expensive so I've been putting aside every penny I can. I wanted to give them all of that, but they wouldn't let me. They think I should buy a condo. Maybe they're right. I just…"

She realized she was rambling. "Sorry. The point is, I need the money."

Rafiq stared at her.

"What?" she asked, carefully running her tongue over her teeth to see if she'd gotten a piece of food caught in them.

"You wish to repay your parents for the wedding?" he asked.

"Of course. It was thousands of dollars for nothing. I'm the one who picked Eric. I'm the one who wanted to marry him. So this is my responsibility."

Her parents had disagreed that it was her fault, but it wasn't as if they were rolling in money. Her dad would be retiring in a few years and her mother had only ever worked part-time.

"And while we're on the subject," she said. "If we do this, I don't want work to be weird. We'd need to keep our personal life separate from work. People will probably find out but I'd rather we didn't flaunt things."

"I agree."

"And when it's over, you can't fire me."

"I give you my word. Should working together be too uncomfortable, I would help you find another position that was to your liking. If you stay here, we will never mention the affair again."

Fair enough, she thought. "It won't be uncomfortable for me," she said. Being his mistress was about her wanting revenge, not finding a new boyfriend. Still, this was by far the most surreal experience of her life. "I'll be fine."

"How flattering," Rafiq murmured.

"What?"

"Nothing. In addition to our sexual relationship, I would expect you to accompany me to various social events."

"That's the part I'm most looking forward to," Kiley told him with a smile. "I want to be seen and have word get back to Eric."

Rafiq's expression didn't change, but she had the feeling she'd said something wrong. She ran over her statement. Oh. Yeah. Maybe that wasn't the most flattering thing to say.

"Of course, I'm really excited about sleeping with you," she added, feeling both embarrassed and uncomfortable.

"I can see that."

She wanted to bang her head against the desk. "Have I blown it completely?"

"No. You offer something unique. An honest relationship in which we both get what we want. There is no pretense of more-tender feelings."

"And you're okay with that?"

"Perfectly. I would think a time period of three months would satisfy both of our needs."

"Sounds good to me," she said. In three months Eric was bound to find out about the affair. She could only hope that the news would devastate him as much as learning the truth about him had devastated her.

"Good." He stood. "Then there is only one more detail to be worked out."

"You mean you're seriously considering me?"

She couldn't believe it. Coming to Rafiq had taken all the courage she had and then some. Relief now combined with her sleepless nights and emotional pain and left her light-headed.

"Yes." He walked around the desk and held out his hand to her.

She stared at it, then at him. He obviously wanted her to take his hand.

"Why me?" she asked, not yet ready for actual physical contact. "I'm not your usual type."

His dark gaze settled on her face. "That is part of the appeal. You would present a unique perspective on the male-female relationship. I find you attractive. I believe you will be my mistress with the same efficiency that you use here at the office. Which means there is only one question left unanswered."

She set her pad on his desk and placed her fingers against his palm. She had an impression of warm skin and strength as he gently pulled her to her feet.

He towered over her, and she had on pretty high heels. He smelled clean, just soap and man, and even though it felt strange to have him continue to hold her hand, it was more good-strange than bad-strange.

His dark eyes seemed to see down to the very depths of her being, as if he could read all her secrets. Not a good thing, she thought. She wasn't the secret type and anything he found down there would be pretty pitiful.

She drew in a deep breath. "What's the question?"

"This," he said, and lowered his head.

She hadn't thought he would kiss her. Maybe she should have. After all, she was offering to be his mistress, which meant an impressive level of physical intimacy, and kissing was the first stop on that road. But here? At the office? In the afternoon?

As his mouth gently brushed against hers, he tugged on her hand and drew her closer. She didn't know what to think, what to feel. She'd been numb since discovering Eric with that woman, so she doubted she was going to be able to respond to Rafiq's kiss.

Only, she had to. This was the final test to see if she was mistress material. As she knew deep in her heart she wasn't; she was going to have to fake it. But how?

Frantic thoughts raced through her mind. She felt awkward standing there, not sure what to do with her arms, her hands. Should she embrace him? Should she go for a wildly enthusiastic tongue kiss? Should she grab his free hand and put it on her breast?

Rafiq raised his head. "You have very noisy thoughts," he murmured.

"Can you hear them?"

"Not the specifics, but the general rumble. You are free to change your mind."

Meaning she didn't have to be his mistress. She knew that. "I want to do this."

He stepped back and sat on the edge of his desk. "Chemistry is important in circumstances such as these."

"What with sex being the point," she said, aware that so far they'd yet to create even a spark, let alone a passionate fire.

"Is that what you think?" he asked. "That the whole point is sex?"

"Isn't it?"

He studied her for several seconds. "Perhaps *you* would like to kiss me."

Oh! Wow. Kiley drew in a deep breath. It hadn't actually been her first choice, but she could guess why he would suggest it. If she couldn't kiss him, she certainly couldn't do anything more interesting.

"I would like to," she said as much as to convince herself as him.

He sat without moving, although he watched her. She had the sense of being stalked, which was crazy. Rafiq wasn't dangerous. Not exactly. He was powerful and good-looking. A great body. Eric was a little on the skinny side, but Rafiq had serious muscles.

Rafiq was a man who knew women—he'd had plenty and they'd all been reluctant for the affair to end. Some had called her to beg her to put in a good word for them.

Some had talked about his prowess in bed. Some had accused her of being the other woman.

She'd wondered about him, of course. He was a fabulously wealthy, handsome prince who had been involved with some of the most beautiful women in the world. What, exactly, was he like in his personal life?

But that musing had been curiosity, not the interest Eric had accused her of. Funny how many times she'd defended herself against the very actions she was about to take.

She moved closer, slipping between his parted thighs and placing her hands on his upper arms. She felt the crisp coolness of his cotton shirt and the heat and strength of his body below. He stayed relaxed and didn't try to hurry her. A faint smile drew the corners of his mouth upward. Then, with her eyes fluttering closed, she leaned in and kissed him.

His lips yielded slightly but did not part. She kept the kiss brief and chaste before moving to the left and lightly kissing his cheek. It was early enough in the day that his skin was still smooth, but she felt the hint of stubble that would arrive later.

She rubbed his cheek with hers, then kissed his jaw and the small spot right below his ear. Some tension inside of her uncoiled a little. Breath flowed more easily. She returned to his mouth, and this time she tilted her head and pressed her lips against his with more enthusiasm.

He responded but didn't try to deepen the kiss. Instead he put one hand on the small of her back. The warm pressure gave her the courage to wrap her arms around his neck and lightly brush her tongue against his bottom lip.

He parted for her. She had the brief thought that she hadn't kissed another man in five years. Only Eric. Then curiosity and a wave of pleasure had her slipping her tongue inside to explore what he offered.

He tasted of coffee and something sweet. His heat surprised her, as did his restraint. He let *her* touch *him.* She was the one who discovered the smoothness of the inside of his lower lip. She sought out his tongue and brushed it with her own.

The hand on her back never moved. He neither urged her forward nor suggested retreat. Not sure what to do next, she broke the kiss, dropped her arms to her sides and straightened. He did the same.

Rafiq's dark expression hadn't changed. No one walking in at this moment would guess anything unusual had happened. Yet Kiley felt a deep shift in the rotation of the universe.

She'd liked kissing Rafiq. Okay, maybe she hadn't seen stars, but she was still dealing with a lot of stuff. The fact that she'd felt anything at all was pretty amazing.

"Do you think we will suit?" he asked.

She was more than a little shocked by the fact that she'd been the one kissing him. "Yes."

"As do I. We will begin tonight. I will send my car for you at seven. You will spend the evening with me at my house. We will share dinner and work out the final details." He glanced at his watch. "I have a conference call in fifteen minutes. If you will get me the file?"

Kiley nodded, grabbed her pad and walked out of his office. As she stood by her own much-smaller desk, she had the sudden urge to break into hysterical laughter. Be careful what you wish for, she thought, not sure if she should celebrate or run for the hills.

Now that she had won the handsome Prince Rafiq of Lucia-Serrat, however temporarily…whatever was she going to do with him?

Chapter Two

Kiley wasn't sure what she should wear on her first night as mistress. Honestly, she couldn't even think the question without wanting to giggle like a teenager or throw up from sheer panic. Second thoughts didn't describe her roller coaster of emotion. Fear, excitement, worry and the pressing need to scream. A mistress? Her? She was the most normal woman on the planet. Her idea of wild living was to pay for a pedicure instead of doing it herself. How could she seriously consider being Rafiq's mistress?

And yet she had. She'd offered and he'd accepted and sometime very soon they were going to have sex.

She couldn't imagine it. Not with Rafiq. Not with any man, really. She'd thought about being intimate with Eric, but that was different. She hadn't worried about anything. She'd known he would be gentle and loving and exciting.

"Talk about wrong," she said aloud as she studied the contents of her closet. Eric had turned out to be Toad Boy and was out of her life forever. Now she was the soon-to-be mistress of a fabulously wealthy sheik prince. A thought she couldn't seem to wrap her mind around.

Not that she wasn't grateful he'd agreed to help her out. She intended to enjoy every moment of her revenge. That goal probably made her a bad person, but she was willing to live with it. The condition of her soul was a little less worrying at this moment than what to wear.

She had plenty of work clothes and tons of casual stuff—jeans, shirts, khaki skirts. But no real mistress wear. Not that she could identify mistress wear. It wasn't as if there was a section on it in InStyle magazine. But she had a feeling jeans and a cotton blouse weren't going to cut it and she didn't want to wear an outfit Rafiq had seen at the office.

After flipping through every item on a hanger, she settled on a simple blue short-sleeved dress and high-heeled sandals. She'd fake-tanned the previous week for her wedding, and there was still enough color on her legs that she didn't have to worry about pantyhose. Earrings and a quick application of lip gloss completed the look.

She still had a few minutes until the car was due to arrive. Kiley walked into the living room of her apartment and spent the time packing up what few remaining wedding presents she had yet to return.

Touching items she and Eric had picked out and put on their gift registry made her sad. Where had things gone wrong? What clues had she missed? Okay, her friends telling her Eric had hit on them was a big one. Why hadn't she listened?

"I'll take responsibility for being stupid about that," she murmured as she closed the box and picked up packing tape. "But not for what he did. He was the cheating, lying jerk in all this, not me."

She heard a car pull up and glanced out the window. Sure enough, there was a large, black limo right there in front of her door. As it was unlikely to be for any of her neighbors, Kiley put down the packing tape and picked up her purse.

Five minutes later she'd met Arnold, the very nice driver, and had been escorted to the huge back seat of the vehicle. The only other time she'd been in a limo had been for her high school prom, and she and her date had been one of the three couples sharing it. This was very different.

There was a bar, a TV and enough floor space for a Pilates workout. "This is so not like my world," she murmured as she buckled up.

A voice in her head asked if she knew what on earth she was doing. Kiley was ready to go with no on that one. She didn't. Not really. Being a mistress was an intellectual concept she didn't want to think about. *Actually* being one, in the flesh, so to speak, was a very scary reality she wasn't prepared to deal with. Although she would have to later that evening.

"I went to Rafiq," she reminded herself. "I'm the one who wanted this. Wanted him."

And she still did. Revenge was all she had left.

Traffic was surprisingly light for a workday evening,

and less than forty minutes later the limo drove down a long, narrow driveway that opened up in front of a wood-and-glass single-story house.

Tropical plants lined the walkway and provided a shaded entry. High walls on both sides offered privacy. When Arnold opened the rear door of the car, Kiley could hear the sound of the ocean.

"Have a nice evening," he said as she smiled at him. "I'll be waiting to take you home when you're finished."

Finished with what, she wanted to ask but didn't. Better not to know for sure.

She walked along the flagstone path to the huge double doors. Before she could find the bell and press it, the door opened and Rafiq stood in front of her.

He might have spoken. She wasn't sure. His lips moved, so there was probably sound, but she didn't hear it. She couldn't think, could barely breathe as she stared at him.

He wasn't in a suit. She'd known Rafiq for more than two years, and she'd only ever seen him in a suit. Usually without the jacket. He took that off as soon as he arrived at work and rarely put it on except for certain clients. She'd seen him tired, cranky, mussed, with his sleeves rolled up and his tie pulled off, but she'd never seen him dressed casually.

Tonight he wore tailored slacks and a polo shirt. The latter told her that her first impression about his body had been correct—plenty of lean muscle sculpted into something darned close to male perfection.

She'd known she was out of her league, based on the women he was usually involved with. Now she realized she was out of her league because of the man he was. Talk about a bad idea.

He was rich, royal and dangerous. He was also gorgeous.

She bit back the need to apologize for taking up his time and scurry back to the limo to be taken home. She'd asked, he'd been interested, and the decision had been made. For reasons clear to no one, Rafiq had wanted her as his mistress. As soon as she stopped hyperventilating, she was going to accept that truth and deal with it.

"Are you all right?" he asked.

She managed a smile. "Not even close, but I'll get better."

"What will help?"

"The passage of time or a head injury."

He smiled. "Perhaps some champagne."

"A possible alternative," she said as he led the way from the foyer into a step-down living room.

Seeing a casually dressed Rafiq had been one shock. Seeing the Pacific Ocean spread out before her like a fabulous painting was another. Floor-to-ceiling windows covered the entire west wall of the living room. She could see a deck, then a bit of sand, then moving, swirling beautiful blue ocean.

"Love the view," she said.

"I'm glad. It reminds me a little of Lucia-Serrat. My house on the island there overlooks the Indian Ocean."

"Is there a difference?"

He crossed to a glass-topped sofa table where a bottle of champagne sat in an ice bucket and a tray of appetizers nestled by two white plates.

Rafiq picked up the bottle and opened it. "The smell," he said at last. "The sound of the ocean is the same, but if I close my eyes and breathe deeply, I can always tell where I am. At home, the salt air is more tropical."

"While here it smells like Hollywood," she said, accepting the slender glass he offered.

"Is that the scent?"

"I'm only guessing," she said, staring at the bottle of Dom Perignon. Sure, she'd had champagne before but never anything *this* expensive. "I know in my head that Lucia-Serrat is a beautiful tropical island, but whenever I think of your part of the world, I picture sand and oil."

"There is that, as well," he said, gesturing to the sofa. "You are imagining traditional desert images. You can find the reality of that in El Bahar or Bahania."

She doubted visiting either country was going to be on her near-term to-do list. First she had to get her life back in order.

"You're related to the royal family of Bahania, aren't you?" she asked.

He waited until she'd settled on one end of the sofa and took the other for himself. "The king of Bahania and my father are cousins."

"An interesting extended family."

She tasted the champagne and was pleased by the light, bubbly flavor. "This is nice," she said.

"I'm glad you're enjoying it. Would you like something to eat?"

"No, thanks."

Food? Now? *So* not a good idea. She was already nervous. Eating would only upset her stomach, which could lead to an unfortunate throwing-up incident. Not a memory she wanted for her first visit to Rafiq's house.

Oh, God. She was in his house! She'd agreed to be his

mistress! Soon there would be nudity and sex and possibly bad language. Her life had become an R-rated movie.

She set down the glass and tried to think of something to say. Funny how she and Rafiq had never run out of things to talk about at the office. Of course there they had business to discuss and now they didn't. Somehow it didn't seem right to bring up the latest oil reserves or mention the meeting he would attend in the morning. She needed a slightly more "mistressy" topic. But what?

And how were they going to do it? Did he just make a move on her and she let him? Was there a universal question or signal she was supposed to pick up, because if there was, she was unlikely to get it.

"I can hear you thinking again," he said with a smile. "You are nervous."

"Wouldn't you be?"

"Under the circumstances?" He considered the question, then said, "Yes."

"Okay, then."

"Perhaps if we discussed logistics you would feel more comfortable."

She doubted anything would help but, hey, stranger things had happened. "Okay. Let's talk."

"I have several upcoming social events I would like you to attend. I will get you a list of dates. In return, if there's anything you want me to do with you, I will."

Her sister was about to give birth, and after the baby came, there would be a big family get-together. Somehow she couldn't imagine taking Rafiq to the party.

"I'll keep that in mind," she said.

"Why are you smiling?" he asked.

"Am I?" She shrugged. "Honestly, I can't see you fitting in with my family. Everyone is very normal. We're your basic hearty, peasant stock. Not a drop of royal blood anywhere."

"Why would that matter?"

"I doubt it's what you're used to."

"I adjust very well to different circumstances."

She angled toward him. "I'm one of three girls. The youngest, in fact. My father is a firefighter. My mom works in a gift store. They've been married thirty-one years and have lived in the same house for nearly twenty of them. It's a four-bedroom ranch-style built in the seventies."

"What is wrong with that?" he asked.

She laughed. "Nothing. My point is, you don't have a 'bondy story' to go with mine. What are you going to say? That the smallest family castle only has eleven bedrooms?"

"I believe it has fifteen, but I've never counted." Rafiq stared into Kiley's blue eyes and liked the amusement he saw there. "But I understand your point. We come from different worlds."

"I'm thinking it's more like different planets."

"Yours sounds very nice."

"It is," she said. "But yours has better jewelry."

He chuckled. "That is true."

She reached for her glass of champagne and took a sip. He watched her and knew the exact moment the humor faded and the nervousness returned. Her grip on the glass tightened and she refused to look at him.

"Kiley, we will not be making love tonight."

Her relief was nearly as tangible as the building itself. Tension dropped from her body, as she sagged back against the sofa. "Really?"

"We need to get to know each other first." He was amused by her reaction. Did she really think he intended to take her so quickly? Much of the pleasure lay in the anticipation, in watching her move and imagining her hands on his bare skin. In listening to her voice and knowing how it would sound when she begged him for more.

"Okay. Good point," she said. "It's just I've never done anything like this before. Obviously. In addition to the whole never-been-a-mistress-before thing, there's the fact that I'm not all that good with men." She wrinkled her nose, then took another sip of the champagne. "I didn't date much in high school. I was more the buddy type."

The information didn't surprise him. While Kiley was very attractive, hers was a more-subtle beauty. Still, the flower one must discover was more special than the one simply thrust in one's path.

"You met Eric in college?" he asked.

"My senior year. We were friends for a while, then we started dating. There were a couple of guys before him but no one special."

The women in his life were usually much more experienced. Not that Rafiq minded her relative innocence. "As I said, we will get to know each other," he told her. "Progress leisurely." He paused, then said, "I assume Eric was your only lover?"

He didn't mind the competition, he simply wanted to know how slowly he should move.

Kiley blushed and turned her head. "He, ah…"

"I do not mind if there have been more."

"Yes, well…" She finished her glass of champagne and set it on the coffee table. It was only when she raised her gaze to his that he saw the truth.

Not *more* lovers. *Less.*

She was a virgin.

Rafiq was less startled by the news than by the fierce need to possess her that swept through him. The primitive emotions startled him with their intensity. In his day-to-day life, he rarely felt his desert heritage, but at that moment he was one with his ferocious history.

"I know it's really old-fashioned, especially now," she said, speaking quickly. "Socially, it's not something I really talk about. I don't even know where the idea came from. My mom always talked about the first time being with someone I loved, but never that I should wait. Still, I wanted to. I wanted to give that to the man I married. I wanted to be a virgin on my wedding night."

She stared at the floor. "Eric knew, of course. He was all for it, the bastard. In a way that's what made it worse. I'm not a saint or a sexless creature. We would kiss and touch and I wanted to do more. I thought I was being strong and noble, and sometimes it was really tough. I thought he believed, too. Instead I would go home frustrated and he would head off to sleep with somebody else."

Rafiq had never had an opinion on Kiley's fiancé until she told him what he'd done. Then he'd felt mild annoyance and contempt. Now he wanted to hunt down the other man and horsewhip him into a bloody pulp. How dare he reject such an incredible gift with thoughtless callousness?

"It is better you didn't marry him," he said, careful to keep his anger from his voice.

"Agreed. He was a jerk and I'm lucky I found out before the wedding." She looked into her glass. "I just don't feel very lucky. I feel stupid. Like I did this really big thing and no one noticed or cared."

Her admission of innocence made him want her more. He wanted to be the first to touch her and pleasure her in the unique way a man could please a woman. But to defile a virgin...

"You must reconsider our arrangement," he told her, even as he longed to pull her close and take her. "Someone who was willing to wait so long should not give her gift so easily."

She stared at him. "You've changed your mind? But you can't."

"I have not," he said gently, hating the need to do the right thing. His body told him to take what was offered without question, but his soul demanded Kiley make the choice. "You said yourself you should be in love the first time."

"Were you?"

He smiled. "It is different for a man. We are eager to dispose of our virginity."

"Gee, that's what I'm thinking. I want this, Rafiq. I wouldn't have asked you if I didn't."

Honor demanded he give her an out. Now that he had and she'd refused it, he wouldn't ask again. "Then we will go on as planned," he said. "With one small change."

She frowned. "What's that?"

"I had thought we would wait a few days to become intimate. Now I think we will move even more slowly."

"You don't have to because of me."

"Oh, but I do." He moved closer and touched her cheek. Her skin was smooth and soft.

Based on what he'd heard about Eric, Rafiq would guess the other man hadn't been interested in teaching Kiley the possibilities.

"There are many ways for a man to please a woman," he said, staring into her eyes. "We will explore all of them together. I will show you the way it should be, and when you are ready, we will be lovers."

Kiley felt equal measures of relief and disappointment. On the one hand, she appreciated that she didn't have to get naked right this moment. On the other hand, there was something about Rafiq that intrigued her.

Maybe it was the way he talked—speaking of possibilities and pleasure. Moving slowly toward an ultimate goal. A shiver of anticipation raced up her spine. Maybe this was going to be fun.

"Would you like to see the house?" he asked. "There are some beautiful pieces I brought from Lucia-Serrat."

The change of topic left her blinking. Couldn't they keep talking about how great he was going to make it? Unfortunately there was no way she could ask, and as he stood, she would guess he hadn't read her mind.

"That would be nice," she said.

She accepted the hand he offered and let him pull her to her feet.

"This small chest was built in the sixteenth century," he told her, pointing at a small, carved chest by the end of the sofa. As he spoke, he rested one hand on the small of her back and placed the other on her upper arm.

Both points of contact were warm. Nice, she thought. More than nice. Interesting. Appealing. He moved his fingers back and forth, stroking her like a cat. As he continued to tell her the history of the chest and touch her, she found herself relaxing.

They circled the living room. He pointed out several works of art painted by people even she recognized. They passed through a large, well-appointed kitchen filled with the delicious scent of cooking dinner. Rafiq pointed to the oven.

"Sana, my housekeeper, has left us dinner. Are you hungry?"

As he asked the question, he put his hand back on her hip. She found herself wanting to step closer. How odd. Until this morning they'd never touched, except by accident as she passed a file or they walked together down the hall. Now he had the right to touch her whenever he wanted, and she could place her hand on him.

"Kiley?"

"What? Oh, dinner. Let's wait a bit. If I eat when I'm too nervous, really bad things happen."

He chuckled. "We don't want that."

"No."

She looked at him, at his broad shoulders and the thickness of his chest. Hard muscles under warm skin. What would he be like to touch?

"What are you thinking?" he asked.

She looked at his face. "That these are very unusual circumstances. When two people date, things start out slowly. Hand holding, then kissing and so on. With a few words we've given each other permission to do whatever we'd like, physically."

"What would you like to do?"

She laughed. "I'm not sure. It's just that I can. Does that make sense?"

"Yes. What would you like to do?" he asked again.

What would she?

She turned so she stood directly in front of him, then raised her hand to cup his cheek. The skin was smoother than it had been earlier when she'd kissed him.

"You shaved," she said, more than a little surprised.

"Yes. I grow a heavy beard and didn't want to scratch you."

Because he'd assumed they would kiss. He hadn't wanted her to be uncomfortable. She wasn't sure why she found the thoughtful gesture so intriguing, but she did. Maybe it was because he'd imagined them kissing. Had the idea been fleeting or had he considered it for some period of time? Did he feel anticipation? He did want her?

Her stomach clenched at the thought. Right now a man wanting her seemed very important. If Eric had ever wanted her, he'd managed to keep his feelings to himself. Or perhaps he'd simply burned them up in another woman's bed.

She lowered her hand from his cheek to his chest and splayed her fingers. He was as hard as she'd imagined. Sculpted. She had a sudden vision of touching his bare skin and her breath caught.

"The tour," she said, stepping back. "What's next?"

He stared at her for several seconds before taking her hand. "The bedrooms."

Oh, goody.

As they went down the hall, Rafiq pointed out several pictures. She saw a photo of his father, the crown prince of Lucia-Serrat, and one of Rafiq dressed for riding. He stood next to a beautiful horse. There were more paintings and objets d'art, a few antiques and a tapestry. He pointed out his home office, a very-well-equipped gym, a lavish guest room and then they stepped into what could only be the master bedroom.

A massive bed dominated the large, open space. Dark, carved furniture made the room seem masculine but not unwelcoming. There was a deck that overlooked the ocean, a low dresser, an armoire and a beautifully framed mirror hanging directly across from the door.

She could see herself in it, with Rafiq behind her. He was tall, several inches above her own five foot seven, and dark to her blond. They looked good together, if slightly wicked.

His eyes met hers in the mirror. She found herself caught in his gaze, thinking how handsome he was and how, just twenty-four hours ago, she could never have imagined herself in this exact position. Here. In his bedroom. Watching him watch her.

He put his hands on her shoulders, then bent down and lightly kissed the side of her neck.

Her entire body erupted in goose bumps as she both felt and saw the tender caress. His lips barely grazed her skin, but the warm, soft contact was enough to make her want to turn in his arms and beg for more. When he straightened, she found she'd stopped breathing and she had to consciously force herself to draw in a breath.

"Perhaps we should see about dinner," he said, his voice low and sensual.

Dinner? Oh, yeah. That evening meal she'd been too nervous to eat before. The good news was she wasn't nervous anymore. The bad news was she hadn't just jumped into the deep end of the pool, she'd taken a flying leap into the middle of the ocean.

Chapter Three

"You completed college with two degrees?" Rafiq asked as he poured Kiley more wine. It had taken her most of the meal to drink the first glass. He knew she didn't smoke, it seemed she barely drank and, based on her bright, cheerful, early-morning demeanor, she didn't party.

"Business and early-childhood development." She pushed a slice of chicken around on her plate. "Odd combination, I know."

"Not if one plans to open a day-care facility."

She looked at him and smiled. "You're right. I'd never thought of that. I love kids. Honestly, I never wanted much more than to be a wife and mother. The business degree was so I could get a good job, and the other studies were to help me to be a good mother. Although, my mom didn't study anything and she was the best. I want to be just like her."

Kiley nibbled on a slice of carrot. "You're probably disappointed."

He'd always known she was intelligent, so her multiple degrees didn't surprise him. She'd carried her half of the conversation at dinner and she continued to surprise him.

"What exactly would have disappointed me?" he asked.

"Me being a secretary and wanting to be a mother. Not very big aspirations. A lot of my friends were shocked when I admitted it to them. They think I should be more. Do more. I guess I feel guilty. These days women are supposed to have it all. But I don't want it all. I just want a little house with a garden and a couple of kids and a man who loves us as much as we love him."

He had been born into royalty, so not many of his acquaintances shared his lifestyle, but Kiley was farther removed than most.

He'd never longed for a small house with a garden. While a wife and children were in his future, the assumption that he would one day marry and father children was far more about providing his country with an heir than any personal desire on his part.

She put down her fork and leaned toward him. "I know that I shouldn't care about what other people think, or the expectations of our society in general, but sometimes it bugs me."

Her expression was earnest, her blue eyes wide and intent. The soft light from the chandelier brought out the strands of gold in her hair. She was beautiful and sincere and he could honestly say he'd never had a conversation like this with a woman he intended to seduce.

"Do you spend much of your day worrying about the expectations of society?" he asked.

"No. Just sometimes." She shook her head. "I'm guessing you can't relate to any of this. You knew who and what you were from the time you were born. Is that a good thing?"

"It simply is, for me. I haven't imagined another life. What would be the point?"

"Plus you're really rich and can pretty much do what you want. That has to be a good thing."

"It is."

She smiled. "So you're not married, right? I just realized I never asked about a Mrs. Rafiq sequestered back on the island."

"I wouldn't be here with you tonight if I was."

"Really?" She sounded surprised. "You'll be faithful when you're married?"

"Do you question me specifically or all men in general?"

"I guess the whole fidelity issue is a sore spot for me, but right now I'm asking about you specifically."

"I'm faithful now."

"With very short-term relationships. Marriage is forever. At least it's supposed to be."

"The expectation for me is that my wife and I will only be parted by death."

"And you'll be faithful all that time?" she asked.

"Of course."

"You're going to have to be really sure you love her."

Love? As if that mattered. "My choice will be based

on more practical matters. She will be the mother of my children."

"But if you don't love her…"

Rafiq found it intriguing that, after all she had been through, she was still a romantic. "Respect and shared goals often last longer than love."

Kiley didn't look convinced. "So, is there a place one goes to find a woman fit to be a princess? Like a princess store?"

Her eyes were bright with humor and the corners of her mouth curved up.

"There's an Internet site," he said, pretending to be serious.

"Oh, I'd love to see it. Do you type in specifications? Height, weight, number of sons required."

"Of course. Along with how many languages I want her to speak and what accomplishments she should have."

"You really need to get going on that," she said with a smile. "So you aren't too old when your kids are born. You want to be able to play ball with them."

"I have a few good years left."

"I don't know. You're over thirty."

"By a year."

"Still. You're looking a little creaky."

"How charming," he said dryly. He liked that she was feeling comfortable enough to joke with him.

"How many children do you want?" he asked.

"Three or four. I was one of three and it was great. There was always someone to play with, and with three of us, the blame for whatever bad thing we'd done could get spread around."

He could see her in a small house, raising her children, working in the garden. She would bake cookies and sew Halloween costumes, and ask for almost nothing for herself. He could imagine birthdays and Christmases when the children would receive piles of presents and there would only be one or two for her. But she wouldn't mind, because her world would be defined by her family.

He studied the gold hoop earrings she wore and the delicate chain around her neck. Modest pieces at best. She would look good in jewels, he thought. Sapphires. The traditional blue stones would match her eyes. He would like to see her in pink sapphires as well. And diamonds. Diamonds and nothing else.

The image of a Kiley wearing only diamonds filled his mind. Desire licked through him, heating his blood. He enjoyed the sensation, even knowing he would not have her for some time. In this case, anticipation would sweeten the union.

"I have been invited to a fund-raiser on Friday evening," he said. "The event is formal and I would very much like you to attend with me."

"Sure." She wrinkled her nose. "How formal?"

"Black tie."

"I've never been clear on what that meant, but I get the general idea. The only really fancy dress I have is my wedding dress, and that would probably be tacky to wear, huh?"

As soon as she spoke, she covered her mouth with her hand. "Oh, no. Is it okay that I said that? Are you offended?"

"It was your wedding, Kiley. You may speak of it as you wish."

"Good. Either way, the dress isn't a good idea. I'll come up with something. I need to take off a little early one day this week to get to the post office and ship back the rest of the gifts. I'll go shopping after that."

Dismantling a wedding sounded like as much work as putting it together, he thought. "Where were you and Eric going to live?"

"We rented an apartment together. The lease doesn't start until the end of the month and we'd discussed maybe painting it before moving in, so I haven't given notice at my place, fortunately." She sighed. "I have to break the lease on the new place, which won't be fun."

"I'll take care of it," he said.

She looked at him. "I appreciate the offer, but it's not your responsibility."

"You are right. It's Eric's. But he is not here and I am. Besides, now you are *my* responsibility."

"Is this a mistress perk?"

He smiled. "One of many."

A faint flush darkened her cheeks. "Are you going to get all imperious if I say I want to do it myself."

"Absolutely. I do imperious very well."

She laughed. "Okay, then I'll give in graciously and say thank you. It's really nice of you to offer, and to be honest I wasn't looking forward to making that call."

"Now you don't have to."

Kiley had no idea why Rafiq had taken on the chore. Under other circumstances she would wonder if he was going to pass it on to his staff, but this time she doubted it. After all, she was part of that staff, and as his secretary, she would know.

"Have you finished?" he asked, nodding at her plate.

"Yes. It was delicious." And she'd eaten more than she'd thought. Funny how once they got talking, she forgot to be nervous.

He stood, walked around the table and waited until she stood. Then he put his hand on the small of her back and guided her through the living room, out onto the deck.

The sun had set some time before, so the ocean was barely visible. She could see the faint white of the waves as they crashed into the shore and, in the distance, lights from another house. He moved in close behind her and wrapped his arms around her waist, drawing her against him.

The night was cool; the man, warm. She liked the feel of him pressed against her, liked the way he held her close.

"I enjoyed dinner," she said. "We have a lot to talk about."

"Are you surprised?"

"A little. I thought things might be awkward, but they're not. Why is that?"

"You're intelligent and don't want to talk about clothes and shoes."

She laughed. "Do you get that a lot?"

"You would be surprised how much."

"Then you're in for a treat with me. I promise never to talk about my clothes. They're just not that interesting."

"They would be if you took them off."

The unexpected shift in the chitchat direction made her breath catch. In a single heartbeat she went from enjoying the moment to being hyperaware of the man. His words shocked her, but in a way that made her curious and excited.

"Fear not, Kiley. I meant what I told you earlier. Not tonight. Not for some time. But I will have you."

The low growl of his voice made her shiver. "Will I like it?"

"I will do my best to make sure you do."

As he spoke, he bent down and kissed her neck. He'd done that earlier, in the bedroom. She closed her eyes and remembered how they'd looked standing together, then her mind cleared as her body absorbed the soft brush of his mouth against her sensitive skin.

He kissed her with the slow deliberateness of a man who had all the time in the world. She tilted her head to give him more room and held on to his arms. He worked his way up from the curve where her neck met her shoulder to the sensitive skin just behind her ear.

"What are you thinking?" he asked, his breath tickling her.

"That this is nice. It feels good."

He raised his head and turned her in his arms so that she faced him. Light from the living room spilled out onto the deck and allowed her to see his features. His dark eyes seemed to burn with an intensity she'd never seen before. There was tension in his body but an easy smile on his lips. Funny how she knew so little about him yet she trusted him. She'd asked to be his mistress for the purpose of revenge, but now she found herself anticipating the three months they were to have together.

He touched her face, tracing the shape of her nose, her mouth. He ran his hands down her neck, then across her shoulders to her arms. From there he slipped to her hands, which he took in his.

"You're very beautiful," he murmured.

"Thank you. But not really. The beautiful part, I mean. I appreciate the compliment though."

He studied her face. "I have been with many women. I know of what I speak. Your eyes are large, and the color forever changes. Dark blue, then darker still. Stormy, clear. Your skin is perfection. Your mouth calls to me, begging for kisses."

He raised her right hand and pressed his lips against her palm. She felt *that* tingle all the way down to her toes.

"Every part of you is beautiful."

Okay, maybe this was part of the seduction, but it was working. She felt her knees getting a little weak and her blood zipping along a little faster.

He reached up with one hand and touched her hair.

"Too short?" she asked. "I know most guys prefer long hair, but I like it short. Eric was forever after me to grow it out."

"I like it," he said, sliding his fingers against her scalp and drawing her a little closer.

She went willingly, hoping he would kiss her, because suddenly she needed to be kissing him. She put her hands on his shoulders and shifted that last inch so that her body pressed against his.

His chest was hard and hot against her sensitive breasts. Her thighs lightly brushed his. It was all so…interesting…and she wanted to get moving to the next level. The kissing level.

He smiled. "I sense your impatience."

"Well, there *is* more talking than I'd thought there'd be."

"Are you complaining?"

"A little."

"Just this morning you were uncomfortable with my kiss. I don't want to rush you."

"I'm okay with it now," she said, staring at his mouth. "Completely fine with it. Look how totally fine I am right now."

"Show me."

Kiley hesitated only a second. Her natural shyness battled with the intellectual knowledge that this was a sure thing. Then need overcame reticence as she wrapped her arms around his neck, rose on tiptoe and pressed her mouth to his.

Unlike the kiss from that morning, he didn't wait to respond. He tilted his head and kissed her back, moving with her, teasing, brushing. His hands settled on her hips, holding her against him. The light pressure made her want to shift closer still, although that didn't seem possible. They were already touching from shoulder to knee.

This felt good, she thought as he touched his tongue to her bottom lip and she parted for him. Better than good.

He claimed her with a fiery passion that left her breathless. One moment there'd been gentle, arousing kisses, but the next moment overwhelming desire threatened to consume her.

He swept inside and stroked her tongue with his. Something about the way he touched her, the way he teased and retreated only to take her again and again had her wanting to surrender. Whatever he wanted he could have—as long as he didn't stop kissing her.

She melted against him, wishing she could crawl inside his body. His hands didn't move from her hips even though she silently pleaded with them to touch and discover and knead. Heat flared between her legs; her breasts swelled. She wanted to rub against him. She wanted to suggest they take this inside.

She'd felt wanting before, of course, but never so quickly, and never with someone she barely knew. Except she did know Rafiq—she had for over two years. But not in this way.

Confusion joined with passion to cloud her mind. Not sure what she felt or what she should do, she stepped back.

His dark eyes revealed nothing of his thoughts.

"Rafiq, I—"

"Shh." He pressed his fingers to her mouth. "It's late. I'll have Arnold take you home."

"But…"

He shook his head and kissed her cheek. "I'll see you at the office. I have a business dinner tomorrow night, but I would like to take you out Wednesday evening."

"I'd like that, too."

She would. Not just because of how she felt when he kissed her but because she enjoyed spending time with him. But what had happened tonight?

He escorted her out to the limo before she could figure out how to ask. As she leaned back in the soft leather for the drive home, she closed her eyes and consoled herself with the thought that there would be more. Much more. Three months was a long time and anything could happen.

Kiley wore her favorite silk blouse to work the next day. It was cobalt blue and suited her coloring. She figured she needed all the confidence she could get after the previous night.

What had happened? How could she have reacted so strongly to Rafiq's kisses? She could accept that she'd enjoyed his company, but what about the rest of it? Less than a week ago she'd planned to marry Eric and live with him for the rest of her life.

Maybe it was a post-wedding reaction. She'd been so focused on the path her life was supposed to take. When it hadn't, she'd been set adrift, carried by a current she couldn't control. She was confused, and Rafiq was a familiar and trusted haven.

Okay, that might explain her emotional reaction to him, but what about the sexual one? She'd been so intent on wanting revenge that she hadn't thought past that. She hadn't considered the reality of actually sleeping with him. If she had, she never would have had the courage to talk to him about her being his mistress.

Yesterday she would have assumed she would simply grit her teeth and get through the sex part because it was expected. Now she thought she might be the one hurrying things along in that department.

Which was not like her at all. She'd been comfortable being a virgin for twenty-five years. Why wasn't she more apprehensive about making love with Rafiq?

When no answer popped into her head, she decided to forget the question and concentrate on work. After making coffee and taking a few calls, she settled down to edit a report one of the staff members had put together. She'd barely finished the first page when Rafiq walked in.

"Good morning," he said as he walked by her desk.

"Morning."

It was the same greeting they always exchanged,

only, this time she was hyperaware of him. She could sense the movement of his body, feel his gaze on her. She felt hot and bewildered and shy and not sure what to do with her hands.

"I left the messages on your desk," she murmured as she rose. "I'll bring in coffee."

The familiar routine should have comforted her, but it didn't. Suddenly everything was awkward. Just twelve hours before, she'd been in Rafiq's arms as they kissed. She'd wanted him with a passion that had surprised her. How on earth was she supposed to forget all that and discuss business?

She poured his coffee and carried it into his office, along with her notepad and a pen. She set the cup on the table and took her usual seat across from his desk.

He'd already removed his suit jacket and settled behind his desk. He studied the messages, then returned two to her.

"Schedule meetings for next week," he said. "An hour each. They'll want more. Tell them no."

She made notes. "You have a lunch meeting today."

He glanced at his schedule and nodded. "The reserve report is due this morning."

"I've already told the mail room to send it up to me."

"Very well."

They discussed business for a few more minutes, then Rafiq leaned back in his chair and looked at her. "I would like to take you shopping tomorrow night," he said.

She clutched her notepad. "I don't understand."

"You will need new clothes. There is the fund-raiser Friday night and several other social events coming up."

She'd never shopped with a man before. She didn't

think men ever *liked* to shop with women. Or anyone, for that matter.

"I can shop on my own," she said. "You don't have to—"

"I want to," he said, cutting her off. "Plus, I can explain what will be required for the various events." He smiled. "Believe me, I will enjoy the experience."

"Okay. If you say so."

"I do. Also, I thought we would want to go away for a long weekend in a month or so. Where would you like to go?"

A trip? Just the two of them? Pleasure filled her at the thought. "I'd like that. But I haven't been many places so anywhere would be exciting for me."

"Paris?" he asked.

She blinked. "Wow. Sure. I'd been thinking more on the lines of somewhere within driving distance, but Paris is good."

"Or London."

She grinned. "Hey, maybe you should surprise me."

"I will. You have a passport?"

"Uh-huh. In my sock drawer." It was nearly three years old and every single page was untouched.

"Good."

There was a moment of silence and Kiley realized she should leave. She gathered her pad and pen, stood and walked to the door. When she reached it, she turned back.

"I had a good time last night."

"As did I."

She bit her lower lip, then smiled. "I thought it would be weird, you know? But it was fun. We had a lot to talk about. I didn't expect that. You're great to work for, but honestly, I never really thought of how you'd be outside of the office. You're nice."

"How thrilling."

She held in a laugh. "You don't want me to think of you as nice?"

"Not really."

"Because you're macho and a prince?"

"Something like that."

"Then I won't mention the nice thing to anyone else."

"I would appreciate that."

Chapter Four

After work on Wednesday, Rafiq escorted Kiley to the limo. She hesitated a second before sliding onto the seat.

"What's wrong?" he asked as she shifted several times instead of reaching for her seat belt.

"Nothing serious," she said with a sigh, then grabbed the seat belt. "I'm nervous. It's not a big deal. Right? I mean it's shopping. I've shopped before. Not with you, though."

He smiled. "I assure you the experience will not be that unfamiliar."

"I wish I could believe you," she murmured as she glanced around at the limo. "You have a regular car, don't you? I've seen you in it."

"Yes. I usually drive myself to and from work. However, the trunk is small and there isn't a back seat, so I thought this would be better."

"It certainly made an impression on my neighbors this morning."

He supposed being picked up in a vehicle like this wasn't the normal morning routine for those who lived in her apartment building.

"I thought it would be easier for us to drive together today so we would have one car for this evening," he said.

She nodded. "I agree. It's a great plan." She angled toward him. "It's just that sometimes the difference between your world and my world is pretty startling. You're a prince."

"We have already discussed that."

"I know. It was fine when you were just my boss, but now, it's totally strange. I'm used to seeing princes in movies, mostly as cartoons. Now you're here, in real life." She glanced toward the privacy partition that was in place and lowered her voice. "It's hard to get my mind around. In theory, I could see you naked."

"I hope it is more than in theory."

"You know what I mean."

He did and her concerns amused him. Unlike other women who only wanted him on their arm to show off what they had managed to catch, Kiley wasn't sure she wanted him at all. He was going to have to change her mind about that.

To that end, he reached for her hand and lifted it to his mouth. As she watched, he gently bit the fleshy pad below her thumb, then licked the center of her palm.

"You worry too much," he said as he laced their fingers together. "Think about shopping."

He couldn't be sure, but he thought her breathing might have increased slightly. She shook her head as if to clear it, then faced front.

"Okay," she said. "Shopping. How exactly does that work?"

"I wouldn't have thought this was your first time in a store."

She rolled her eyes. "That's not what I mean. This is my first time shopping with you. I know what you've done with your other women. I've seen the bills."

"Then what questions do you have?"

"Just that I don't really wear a lot of expensive clothes. I'm not sure that I need them."

"The events we will attend require you to dress a certain way. It is my decision to go and therefore the clothes are my responsibility. I know how much I pay you and while the salary is more than generous, it does not cover expenses like these."

She looked at him and narrowed her gaze. "Excuse me? A *more* than generous salary? I earn every penny of that. I work really hard and I'm good at my job and…" She stopped and pressed her lips together.

"Yes?" he promoted.

"You were teasing me."

"That was my original plan."

"Sorry. Okay, so you buy me really expensive clothes. Can we return them in three months so you get your money back?"

"No. You will keep the clothes. Another mistress perk."

She leaned back against the seat. "Except for my father, no man has ever bought me clothes. I'm not in this for the money, Rafiq."

"I'm aware your motives are far more noble."

She considered that. "Is revenge noble?"

"I come from a long line of cruel warriors. It is to me."

"An interesting way of looking at things, but okay. I just want to be sure you understand why I'm doing this."

He leaned toward her and touched her cheek. "I understand completely."

"I don't care about keeping the clothes."

"Perhaps you will change your mind when you see them."

"Unlikely. But I appreciate you doing all this for me."

"A perk," he reminded her

"What are your perks?" she asked.

"You."

"I don't actually consider myself a perk. I'm a sure thing, which may or may not be a plus. I'm not experienced. For all you know, I'll be crappy in bed."

"Unlikely."

"I wish I could be as positive."

"Are you nervous?"

She dropped her gaze. "Of course. When I think about us, you know, doing it."

He smiled. "It will be more than just 'doing it.'"

"Oh." She swallowed and returned her gaze to his. "You have a lot of experience, don't you? I know how many women there have been just since I've been working for you. Doesn't that get old? Don't you ever want more than an endless parade of beautiful, willing women?" She shook her head. "Never mind. I answered my own question."

"The variety is nice."

"Okay. I get that, but what about really knowing

someone? What about feeling connection and a place to belong?"

"That does not come from a relationship. That comes from within." He rubbed his thumb across her mouth. "I say how long. I say when it's over. Then they walk away and I am free."

"So no one gets hurt?"

"I hope they don't," he said. "I make the rules as clear as I can. Sometimes they get too involved and I feel bad about that."

"What about you? Do you ever get hurt?"

"Not so far. I am fairly impervious to most female charms."

"Really?"

He smiled. "Do you take that as a challenge?"

"I can't tell you how much I want to say yes, but I don't think I can. I get nervous just being in your car. But someone, somewhere is going to get to you."

"Do you think so?"

"The law of averages are in my favor."

"Do you want to be there to see it happen?" he asked.

"No. I don't want to see you hurt. Is that what you think of me?"

He studied her blue eyes and the intense honesty he saw there. "No. You worry too much about other people's feelings."

"Not Eric's," she reminded him. "I hope he's feeling horrible, but I doubt it."

He watched the play of emotions as they drifted across her face.

"Are you still sad?" he asked.

"Sometimes. But I thought it would hurt more. I

thought I'd be devastated and I worry that I'm not. I keep telling myself the pain hasn't hit yet."

"Perhaps you were not as in love with him as you thought."

She shook her head. "If that's true, it's not good news. I was going to marry him."

"Love is not required."

"It is in my world. It's bad enough that he treated me like an idiot. If I went through all that and didn't love him, then I'm going to need some serious therapy to get my life on track."

He chuckled, then leaned forward and lightly kissed her. "I always enjoy your perspective on things."

"My sister says I'm twisted."

"Only in a good way."

"I'm not sure that's possible."

She smiled as she spoke. Rafiq realized that he liked Kiley. He'd always thought of her as efficient and attractive, but the more he got to know her as a person, the more he found himself enjoying her company. He could not always say that about the women in his life.

When this was over, he was going to have to do something for her. Perhaps he would buy her a house and pay off the rest of her wedding. Something that would help her future.

But first there was the present—this night and their shopping expedition. He usually found shopping sessions boring, but not this time. Not with her. He had very specific plans to further her seduction.

Kiley had nearly relaxed when the car pulled up in front of a very elegant-looking boutique in the heart of

Beverly Hills. Instantly tension exploded in her stomach, making her midsection ache and her mouth go dry.

She took in the custom awnings, the expensive window displays and the sign for valet parking and knew she was in over her head. Then she saw the Closed sign on the glass front door and nearly giggled with delight.

"Gee, they're not open," she said, trying not to sound delighted.

"To the general public," Rafiq said as Arnold walked around to open the rear door. "I have made special arrangements with the owner."

Bummer. "Do you always come here?" she asked.

"It is one of my favorite stores, but no, there are others I frequent. However, I thought the selection here would suit you best."

"Have you slept with the owner?"

Rafiq looked at her and raised his eyebrows. "Why do you ask?"

She shrugged. "I thought a place like this would be owned by some elegant woman from France or Italy. You know the type—impossibly beautiful with a fabulous accent."

"While Gerald is a delightful gay man, he is not my type, so no. We are merely friends."

Kiley felt the heat on her cheeks and knew she was blushing. Hopefully Rafiq wouldn't notice.

She vowed she would keep her mouth shut at all times and only speak when spoken to. That was the only possible way to get through this. Being Rafiq's mistress had seemed like an easy solution to her problem of how to hurt Eric back, but in reality, it wasn't that simple at all.

He led her into the boutique. The sign might say the store was closed, but the door wasn't locked, and as soon as they stepped inside, they were greeted by a tall, thin, well-dressed man who kissed both her hands and declared her to be completely "precious."

"So much potential," Gerald told Rafiq as he looked Kiley over. "I have the list you sent me and several things already picked out."

Kiley reclaimed her hands and shifted closer to Rafiq. "You sent him a list?"

"Yes. Of events. Via e-mail."

Of course. Otherwise, how would they know what to buy?

"What can I get you?" Gerald asked. "Champagne? Wine?"

Kiley had a feeling that liquor was a bad idea. "I'll have a glass of sparkling water, if you have it."

"Of course."

Rafiq ordered scotch, then leaned close to her. "Sparkling water. You're so wild."

"Hey, I got it with lime."

He smiled at her and in that moment, time stood still. Kiley didn't know what to make of it. Why did one smile matter? But she couldn't help feeling happy and a little floaty as he and Gerald discussed her clothing needs.

She took the glass of sparkling water that one of the sales clerks offered her and nearly choked when she heard the word *lingerie*.

Gerald excused himself to prepare the dressing room. Kiley turned to Rafiq. "Lingerie?"

"Of course."

"But why?" She shook her head. "Never mind. It's

probably a good idea. I buy my stuff on sale. I doubt you'd be impressed."

"It is more about the present than the wrapping, but sometimes the wrapping is nice, too."

She'd never thought of lingerie as wrapping, but she supposed it was. Several minutes later she found herself trying on slacks and blouses, sweaters and boots. There was an entire collection of casual clothes. She put on each outfit and walked out for Rafiq's nod of approval. He often asked her opinion, agreeing when she liked something, telling her not to get it if she didn't.

After a half hour or so of casual wear, she moved into cocktail dresses. There were flirty designs with asymmetrical hems and black silk with beading. These were followed by actual formal gowns.

Kiley found herself zipped into one that was strapless, velvet and flowing. The garment swayed with her movements. The strapless style showed off more than she was used to but she didn't feel exposed. Instead she ran her hands down the velvet clinging to her body and knew this was the one.

"I love it," she said as she burst out of the dressing room and twirled in front of Rafiq. "Isn't it the best? Don't you love the skirt?" She held it out for him, then spun again. "Even the shoes are fabulous." She held out one foot to show the strappy silver sandals Gerald had brought her. "They hurt, but beauty is pain."

Rafiq stood and moved next to her. "So you like it?"

"I love it. But seriously, where exactly am I going to wear something like this?"

"To the fund-raiser on Friday."

"Really? You mean I can get it?"

He smiled. "You are unlike anyone I've known before. So very earnest."

"No. Not earnest. I want to be sexy and exotic and—"

He cut off the rest of her sentence by pulling her close and kissing her. There were no preliminaries this time, no gentle teasing. Instead he claimed her, thrusting into her mouth and taking what he wanted.

Had someone described such a kiss to Kiley, she would have sworn she would hate it, but in reality, she found herself eager to surrender. The act of being taken by a man who knew exactly what he was doing was a short road to pleasure. Blood heated, her thighs trembled, and soon she found herself forgetting about everything but the need to be as close to him as possible.

At last he drew back and rested his hands on her shoulders. "What were you saying?" he asked.

"I haven't got a clue."

"Good. We will take the dress because it was made for you."

He turned her toward the dressing room, kissed her bare shoulder and then gave her a little push.

She moved as if in a dream. Wow, talk about an easy way to cloud her mind and change the subject. He was really good at that whole kissing thing. They should do it more.

But when Kiley walked into the spacious dressing room, she found herself suddenly nervous again. Not because of what Rafiq had done, but because of the lace and silk nightgown hanging directly in front of her.

Oh, my. So, was she expected to, ah, try that on and model it?

She crossed the carpeted floor and stood in front of the lingerie. In theory she could be covered, but the lace didn't leave all that much to the imagination.

Still, this was for Rafiq and he was going to see her naked eventually. She might as well get used to the idea. Besides, so far all their physical contact had been pretty spectacular.

She removed the evening gown and the sandals, then slipped off her strapless bra. As she reached for the nightgown, she would have sworn the lights dimmed just a little.

The silk and lace slid down her body. The cool fabric made her shiver, but not as much as when the door suddenly opened and Rafiq entered the large dressing room.

He seemed taller, bigger and more dangerous. She'd always known he was a man, but at that moment he seemed even more male. Almost predatory.

She had the urge to cover herself, but instead forced herself to stand still, with her chin raised. She wanted this. At least, that was the theory.

His dark gaze swept over her, settling on her face. "You're very beautiful," he said.

"Thank you."

"Do you believe me?"

"I want to."

"You should believe." He took a step closer.

There was something about his eyes, something...

"What are you thinking?" she asked, half afraid of the answer.

"That I want you. I will not take you. Not yet, but I want you."

His words made her tremble, but not with fear. Instead an emotion swept through her—one she couldn't identify right away. And then she knew.

Desire.

She wanted him. While she was nervous and uncertain, she still wanted to know what it would be like to be with him.

He moved close but didn't touch her. Instead he slowly walked around her. "You told me you were a virgin," he said, his voice low. "How far did you and Eric go?"

The question embarrassed her. "Some kissing," she whispered.

He stopped in front of her and touched her cheek. "I only wish to understand how much is familiar and what is new. I want to excite you, Kiley, not frighten you."

Of course. "We, ah, did some touching. You know, he, ah, touched my breasts."

His gaze never left her face. "Anywhere else?"

"A little. Just through clothes."

"Did you touch him?"

"Not, um, there."

"Did you see him naked?"

She swallowed. "No."

"But you do understand what happens between a man and a woman?"

"Yes," she whispered. "I got an A in health class."

He chuckled. "I'm sure you did."

He moved behind her. The dressing room was a circle of mirrors so she could see him as he lowered his head and lightly kissed her shoulder. She saw as well as felt the scrape of his teeth on her skin. Her breasts tightened. The outlines of her nipples were clearly visible.

When he brought his hand around in front of her, she

was sure he was going to touch her there. Instead he rested his palm on her belly and splayed his fingers. She felt the imprint of each one.

Move! She silently screamed at him to shift higher, to touch her breasts. They ached, and she knew that only his touch would make things better. Heat burned her through the silk, but he did not move. Just when she was about to cover his hand with hers and lift him into place herself, he straightened and stepped back.

"We should go now."

"I've never gone through a drive-thru in a limo before," Kiley said as she unlocked her front door and stepped into her ground-floor apartment. "I'm just glad we managed the turn. I'm sure everyone there talked about seeing us."

Rafiq watched as Kiley flipped on lights, then showed Arnold to the bedroom.

"I made room in my closet earlier." She eyed the hanging bags and boxes, then shook her head. "But not enough. We'll be a second," she called to Rafiq. "Make yourself at home."

He did as she requested, moving around the living room, stopping to look at family photographs on a shelf in the corner and above the unit holding the television. There were photos of three girls, obviously sisters, and parents. Pictures from graduations, weddings, and vacations. None that could be Eric, though, he thought.

Arnold and Kiley came out of the bedroom. His chauffeur nodded and left, while Kiley picked up the bags of burgers and fries. "Do you want to eat in here, or in the dining room? Well, it's not a room, really.

More of a nook. But there are chairs and a table. Or we could eat at the sofa. Do you want to watch something on television?"

She still wore the clothes she'd had on at work that day. A narrow skirt and pale-pink blouse, sensible high heels. He preferred her in the nightgown...or perhaps nothing. Yes, that would be his preference. Bare skin.

"Why are you nervous again?" he asked. "I thought you were more comfortable with me now."

"I am. It's not you. It's me and the apartment." She shrugged. "I like it here. The place was built in the 1920s so there are lots of architectural details. I like the high ceilings and arched doorways. But it's still a one-bedroom apartment. You're Prince Rafiq of Lucia-Serrat. Have you even been in an apartment before?"

"Yes. Several times." Although not one like this, he thought. Still, he liked the pretty furniture and the plants that grew in brightly colored pots. "This place suits you."

"Thank you. I like it. No pets, though, and I always wanted a dog. Not that Eric did. Don't you want to eat?"

He shook his head. "I am not hungry, but you go ahead."

"Is it the burger thing? Should we have gone somewhere more upscale?"

"It is not about the food at all."

"Then what's wrong? You seem...restless."

He was. The logical part of him, the civilized man, knew that seduction would be the most pleasurable road for both of them. But the desert warrior wanted to simply take the woman before him. He wanted to know the heat of her embrace, the taste of her skin. He wanted to hear her cries of pleading, then of pleasure, as he coaxed her into surrender.

So he held on, knowing it was too soon and yet still needing that which he could not have.

"I find myself in the unique position of waiting for what I want," he said.

She tilted her head. "I don't understand."

"You."

"Oh." Her eyes widened. "But we have an agreement. I'm a sure thing. You could just…you know. Do it."

He smiled. "As we've discussed. But there is more to being with a woman than the act itself. There is anticipation and then joint pleasure. I'm not interested in getting off, Kiley. I want you to be as ready, as aroused."

Her eyes got bigger and bigger. He moved closer but didn't touch her.

"Besides, there are other pleasures," he told her. "Tonight I enjoyed watching you try on different clothes. I imagined where we would be when you wore them. What we would be doing. Dancing in the ball gown. On the beach with you in shorts."

She stared at him. "The nightgown?" she asked, barely breathing.

"In my bed."

"Is that something you like thinking about?"

"Yes. It makes me want you more."

He reached for her hand and brought it to him. He guided her until her palm pressed against his erection. He kept his touch light, in case she wanted to pull away. Instead she rubbed against the length of him, discovering his hardness.

"All this from thinking about us being together?" she asked.

He nodded.

"What would happen if we kissed?"

Chapter Five

Kiley hadn't meant to kiss Rafiq, but there she was, up on tiptoe, pressing her mouth against his. Something had come over her and she'd given in to the urge. Fortunately, he didn't seem to mind. He kissed her back, moving his mouth against hers.

She put her hands on his shoulders and felt the strength of him. So solid, she thought. So masculine. There was power there, which he kept under careful control. What would happen if he truly let go? Would she be overwhelmed? Swept away? Both thoughts thrilled her.

She wrapped her arms around his neck and leaned into him. He brushed his tongue against her bottom lip as he rested his hands on the small of her back. More, she thought as she parted for him. She wanted more.

Every part of her ached. An unfamiliar wanting made her skin feel too tight. Heat flared within her, moving without purpose, leaving her edgy and impatient.

She circled his tongue with hers, then pressed her lips together and sucked. He tensed in her arms, then nipped at her lower lip.

Was he still hard? she wondered, not exactly sure how to find out. She wanted to press her hips against his, rub with her belly to feel for the thick ridge, but the action seemed too obvious and tacky. Still, touching him had been exciting. To think he could react like that without them doing anything thrilled her. She wanted more. She wanted…

He moved his hands to her waist where he tugged gently on her blouse. The cotton pulled free of the waistband of her skirt. As they continued to kiss, he slid his hands under the fabric until he touched her bare skin.

Excitement filled her. Even as he pulled back enough to kiss his way along her jaw, he slipped his hand around to her waist, then slowly, ever so slowly, up her rib cage.

Yes, she thought, letting her head fall back. He kissed her neck, then nipped her earlobe, and still his hands rose. His fingers moved, his palms brushed. Closer and closer to her breasts. Her body tensed, her nipples tightened so much they ached. He had to touch her. He had to.

And at last he did. He slipped his hands over her bra and cupped her.

It felt good. Better than good. Without thinking, she reached down and began to unbutton her blouse. Her hands brushed against his and she froze as she realized what she was doing. The mood faded and uncertainty set in. She dropped her arms to her sides, opened her eyes and found him watching her.

"I'm sorry," she whispered, not sure what she apologized for.

"Because you were enjoying what I was doing? Because you wanted more?" He reached for her hand and drew her close again. "I would be unhappy if you hadn't liked my caress. It pleases me to touch you. I want it to please you, as well." He put her hand on his chest. "Do you like that?"

She rubbed her fingers against his hard muscles. "Yes."

"Then we are in agreement."

He reached for her blouse and finished unfastening the buttons. Then he bent down. "Want me," he breathed, just before he kissed her.

She surrendered instantly. All doubts faded and she wrapped her arms around him, eager to be closer and feel all of him.

He brought his hands back to her breasts and rubbed her through her bra. He found the front clasp and easily unfastened it. Then he touched her bare skin and it was heaven.

It was all she could do to keep kissing him while he explored her curves. It wasn't that she wanted to stop the kissing, but there was so much to think about and experience. The warmth of his fingers, the way he tickled and teased before finally brushing his thumbs against her tight nipples. The pleasure that shot through her when he rubbed harder there.

More, she thought. More.

He must have heard her because he bent down and pressed his mouth against her breast. Even as his hand continued to touch and stroke and rub, he sucked her nipple, flicked it with his tongue, then sucked again.

She clung to him, barely able to stay standing. Fire shot through her. Need grew until it was all she could think about.

He moved to the other breast and pleasured her there. Her breathing grew ragged. Her panties dampened and her thighs trembled.

"Rafiq," she breathed.

He raised his head and kissed her, then stepped back. His gaze moved to her bare breasts. "So beautiful," he told her, then looked into her eyes. "I will see you in the morning."

"Wh-what? You're leaving?"

He smiled. "It is best. Good night."

Then, before she could grasp what was happening, he walked to the door and let himself out. She was left standing in her living room, half-naked and not quite sure what had just happened. If he was trying to make her want him more, he was doing a really great job.

"The man knows what he's doing," she said as she fastened her blouse. "Thank goodness one of us does."

Friday night Kiley sat in Rafiq's Mercedes SL 600 convertible. The close confines of the car made her very aware of the man next to her. Although, she was starting to think she would be aware of him even if they were at opposite ends of a football field. He'd shown up in a tailored tuxedo, looking elegant and very princely. Just thinking about it made her toes curl.

"You didn't have to let me off work early," she told him as they drove onto the freeway and headed west. "Me being your mistress wasn't supposed to change things between us."

He glanced at her. "Are you complaining because I asked you to work less?"

She smiled. "Is that your way of saying 'shut up and say thank you'?"

"Perhaps."

"Then I will." She looked out the window, then back at him. "This is my first fund-raiser. Is there anything I should know?"

"Not at all. There will be a cocktail hour, dinner, dancing and entertainment. I attend to support the children's hospital and because, as a representative of Lucia-Serrat, it is expected of me. But otherwise it is not how I would choose to spend my evening."

"Me, neither," she confessed. "But being with you is fun."

"Thank you. I enjoy your company as well."

His words made her happy. Funny how she'd been so willing to be his mistress without considering all the intimacies implied in the relationship. Not just that they would be lovers, but also that they would spend time together.

Fortunately, being with Rafiq really was easy and fun. There was also a connection she hadn't expected, which made her wonder how they were going to go back to just working together when the three months were over. Then she reminded herself that it was barely the end of week one of her three-month affair. Perhaps she should not be so quick to anticipate the end.

* * *

They pulled up in front of the large Westside hotel. After the valet helped Kiley out of the low-slung car, she smoothed the front of her dark-blue velvet ball gown.

"Ready?" Rafiq asked as he came around the rear of the car and offered her his arm.

"Absolutely." She felt good. Confident and attractive. It was only after they entered the ballroom that she realized how many people were watching them.

"They're staring," she whispered, trying to keep smiling.

"It's because you're so beautiful," he told her.

"Ha. It's because you're a prince. I'm used to blending in. This is going to take some getting used to."

"Be grateful I didn't bring over any of the really big jewelry."

Even as she laughed, she touched the diamond and sapphire necklace Rafiq had put on her earlier that evening. The sparkling stones had delighted her. Hearing that they were just on loan hadn't diminished her pleasure in wearing something so beautiful.

"The most expensive thing I've ever borrowed before was a pair of shoes from my sister. I guess I'm lucky the jewelry didn't come with security guards."

"The insurance company only requires them when the value is over one million dollars. This is slightly under that."

A million? Dollars? She touched the earrings.

"I'll be really, really careful," she promised.

"Don't worry yourself."

He led her into a massive ballroom decorated in gold, silver and black. Balloons floated overhead, while mirror-covered pillars reflected light. A few hundred well-dressed people filled the space, the sound of their laughter competing with the orchestra.

Rafiq greeted several couples he knew and introduced her. Kiley smiled politely and tried not to wonder what they were thinking. No doubt they were used to seeing him with a different woman every few months. She felt odd, being considered one of his women—not because she minded the association, but because she didn't think she was his regular type.

"Would you like to dance?" he asked. "Or would you prefer to find our table and sit?"

She glanced at the fairly empty dance floor, then back at him. "Can we dance? I took lessons for the wedding so I have some moves." She grinned. "Okay. 'Moves' would be strong, but I think I can follow."

His dark eyes flickered with an emotion she couldn't read. "You and Eric took dance lessons."

"Oh, please. We signed up, and he always had an excuse not to be there. But I was able to practice with other guys there. Am I explaining too much?"

"Not at all."

He guided her to the dance floor and took her in his arms.

"This is nice," she said as he pulled her close and settled his hand on the small of her back. The song was slow enough that she was able to just think about the moment rather than where to put her feet.

"I agree."

His low voice rumbled in his chest.

She closed her eyes and lost herself in the music. Rafiq held her as if she was something precious. She liked how their bodies moved together. The idea of the fund-raiser made her nervous, but being with Rafiq made it worthwhile. Especially the later part. When he took her home.

Anticipation made her breath catch as she thought about them returning to her place. She would invite him in and they would…well, she wasn't exactly sure what they would do, but she was sure it would be exciting. She'd stopped by a gourmet store and had picked up chocolate-covered strawberries to get things going. The price had nearly made her faint, but she'd bought them anyway. Chocolate-covered strawberries sounded exotic and sexy, and Lord knew she needed all the help she could get in both departments.

Although she wasn't sure when they were supposed to eat them. Before they started anything? During? Wouldn't they be sticky in bed?

"You move very well," Rafiq murmured in her ear.

"Thank you. So do you."

"We are well matched."

She liked the sound of that.

"Take a deep breath," he told her.

"What?"

"Take a deep breath. Eric is here."

She heard the words, but they didn't make sense. Eric? "My ex-fiancé?"

"Yes. He just came in. He's alone."

"But he's supposed to be in Hawaii. Our reservation was through Sunday."

Rafiq turned so that she could see the entrance to the ballroom. Sure enough, Eric stood there, looking around.

Everything else faded until she saw only him. Medium height, reddish-brown hair, green eyes. He wore a tuxedo and looked good. She continued to stare, waiting to feel devastated. Surely now her emotions would overwhelm her.

But there was only anger at what he'd done and a strong desire not to have anything to do with him.

"Do you wish to speak with him?" Rafiq asked.

She turned away from Eric and smiled at Rafiq. "No, thanks. I prefer to spend my time with you."

One corner of his mouth turned up. "I must admit, I prefer your company to Eric's, as well."

She laughed. "Gee, that's not much of a compliment."

"How unfortunate, as I meant it as such."

He turned her and they moved back into the growing crowd of dancers.

"Shall I distract you by telling you who else is here?"

"I'd like that."

"There are several television stars. A few from daytime soaps. I shall have to keep you from them so you aren't tempted by their handsome faces."

She looked into *his* handsome face and smiled. "You don't have to worry about that."

"I'm not so sure. These pretty boys can be sly. But if they would challenge me for your affections I would take them all."

"So speaks the desert warrior."

He smiled and joked, but she knew he was only partly kidding. There was a strength to him, a determination. Not that she was interested in anyone else. She'd given her word to be faithful to him for their time together and she would honor that commitment. He made it easy, she thought. Every time he took her in his arms, she couldn't imagine being anywhere else.

Later that evening Kiley excused herself and walked toward the champagne fountain. As she reached for a glass, she felt someone come up behind her.

"Kiley? What are you going here?"

She picked up the glass, then turned and saw Eric next to her.

The last time she'd spoken with him, she'd caught him in bed with another woman. Her first thought was to wonder how she could have been so stupid where he was concerned. Her second was to wish she'd stayed with Rafiq rather than getting something to drink.

"I'm attending the fund-raiser," she said quietly, turning to where Rafiq still stood in conversation with a business associate. "I'm surprised you're not still in Hawaii."

Eric shook his head. "I couldn't stop thinking about you. About us."

"How unfortunate for you."

She started to leave, but he put his hand on her arm. "Wait. You have to listen."

She stared at his hand on her bare skin and waited to feel something. They'd been engaged for three years— there had to be some emotion left.

But there wasn't. Not about Eric, anyway. All she felt was a strong need to return to Rafiq.

Which said what about her? That she hadn't loved Eric? That he'd become a habit? Was it possible? But as much as she searched her heart, she couldn't seem to find anything stronger than bruised pride and anger at being played for a fool.

"I'm talking to you," Eric snapped.

She blinked as she realized he *had* been saying something.

"I guess I'm not interested in listening," she said, and pulled free of his touch.

"Are you with him now?" he asked, pointing at Rafiq.

"Yes."

Eric's eyes narrowed. "I always knew there was something going on between the two of you. Dammit, Kiley, you lied to me."

"I did no such thing. Until Monday morning, he was simply my boss. Of course, all that has changed now."

She had the satisfaction of watching Eric go pale. "You can't be sleeping with him."

"Really? Why not?"

"You're nothing like his other women."

"I suppose that's true, but I'm okay with that."

Eric swore under his breath. "I treated you like a porcelain doll."

"Oh, is that what you call it? From my perspective, you were a lying bastard who cheated on me regularly. It's not my idea of respect or affection."

"We had something great together," he told her.

"That would be my line to you." She took a step back. "You could have had me, Eric, and you blew it completely. Now it's over. Ironically, I'm grateful. A few days away from you have shown me there was a whole lot less to our relationship than I realized." She turned to leave.

He stepped next to her. "Rafiq doesn't give a damn about you. He's just using you for sex."

"Perhaps that has happened in the past, but in this

case, you're wrong. He's not using me for sex. I'm using him."

She thought Eric was going to faint. The color fled his face and his breathing stopped. "You can't be. You were saving yourself for marriage."

"You're right, and look what it got me. Now if you'll excuse me, I must return to my lover."

With that she walked away.

Kiley sipped from her champagne glass and tried not to grin too broadly. But it was hard to act calm when she wanted to race to Rafiq's side and give him a high-five.

She'd faced Eric and had walked away the winner. He hadn't intimidated her or made her feel bad. She'd said what she'd wanted to and then she'd left. It was a huge victory and she felt like celebrating.

But as she approached their table, she saw Rafiq was no longer speaking with an oil executive from Bahania. Instead he was engaged in a very intense conversation with a beautiful woman.

She was petite and perfectly dressed in dark red. A little older than Rafiq, perhaps, but only by a few years.

Kiley stopped and watched them for a few seconds, then headed for the restroom. Her excitement at her victory over Eric faded and in its place was a low pain in her stomach.

She wasn't crazy enough to worry about every conversation Rafiq had with a woman. But there had been something different this time. An intimacy. They knew each other and had for a long time. There was a past between them.

He had demanded fidelity and had promised the same

in return. Had he meant it? Were all men incapable of being faithful, or did she simply bring out that trait in the ones she knew?

Chapter Six

They left the hotel shortly after midnight. Rafiq never liked to stay to the end, and Kiley had seemed pleased when he'd suggested leaving. He wondered at the reasons. Sometime after dinner she'd gotten quiet.

Now, in the silence of the car, he prepared himself to find out what was wrong. In the way of most women, she would at first say nothing. He would be forced to ask again and again until she finally told him. It was a flaw in the female psyche—an inability to state the problem the first time asked.

Often Rafiq simply didn't bother. The pain wasn't worth the reward. But in this case he wanted to know what troubled Kiley and, if possible, fix it.

"You are very quiet," he said. "Did something happen tonight to upset you?"

Was it Eric? She'd told him about her conversation with the other man. At the time he would have sworn she felt nothing for her ex-fiancé, but perhaps she was remembering what could have been.

He didn't like that, but there was little he could do to stop her from missing Eric. Reminding her of what the other man had done to her seemed cruel. He knew Kiley was sensible enough to recover eventually, but selfishly, he wanted her attention now.

"I saw you talking with someone," she said. "A woman. Petite. Beautiful. I told myself it was probably nothing, but the conversation seemed…intimate."

It took him a moment to realize what she was talking about. Had she actually answered his question without prompting? He was so surprised, he nearly missed the point of her words.

"Are you concerned there is a woman from my past who may come between us?" he asked.

"Sort of."

Her honesty surprised him. He recalled the evening and searched for someone who fit her description. There had been no ex-lovers there. No one who could have made Kiley uncomfortable. His conversations had been with business associates and their wives.

Except for one woman.

"Was she a few years older and wearing a red dress?"

Kiley glanced at him. "That would be the one. You know her. You have a past with her. I understand that it's very likely that you'll run into women you've known. I'm not saying you can't be friends with them, but we have an agreement that we'll both be faithful. As you can imagine, I'm a little touchy on the subject. I need to know you'll keep your end of the deal."

Under any other circumstances, he would have laughed, but he was aware of how difficult it had been for her to speak her mind.

"I assure you, I will never be unfaithful to you. I do not give my word capriciously, and once given, it bonds me to the death."

He glanced at her and saw her eyes widen.

"Wow," she murmured. "Okay, then. I guess I have to believe you."

"Even if you did not, I can assure you that the woman I spoke with earlier will never be a threat to you."

"A bad breakup?"

"Not in the way you mean. She is my mother."

He enjoyed the sharp intake of breath, then Kiley's stunned silence. They arrived at her apartment before she could gather her thoughts.

After parking, he escorted her inside and waited while she turned on the lights.

"Would you like something to drink?" she asked. "I have wine in the refrigerator."

"I'll get it," he told her, and made his way into her small kitchen.

Signs of her were everywhere. In the brightly colored curtains at the window, in the stack of books on the kitchen table and the cartoon mug in the sink. He opened the refrigerator and pulled out the bottle of white wine. As he did he noticed a clear plastic container with several chocolate-dipped strawberries and smiled. Did she plan to seduce him later? He must remember to make it easy for her to do so.

When he returned to the living room, she'd kicked off her high heels. He took off his jacket, then settled next to her on the sofa and opened the bottle of wine.

"Tell me about your mother," she said quietly. "If she's here and your father is happily married in Lucia-Serrat, I'm guessing they divorced?"

"They never married." He handed her a glass of wine, touched it with his, then leaned back in the sofa. "Many years ago, she was an actress. She came to the island to film a movie. My father was young, just seventeen and he fell madly in love with her. Or he wanted to sleep with her. At seventeen they can be the same thing. I'm not sure what she felt about him—she never said. I know they had an affair, and I was the result."

Kiley sipped her wine and put the glass on the coffee table. She reached up and unfastened her earrings. "It could have been romantic. Young love, an impetuous relationship that results in a baby."

"It wasn't. My father was too young to marry and *his* father disapproved. My mother pushed hard to be a princess, but when that didn't happen, she agreed to a cash settlement."

Kiley paused in the act of undoing her necklace and looked properly outraged. "Money? She took money for her baby. She let herself be *paid?*"

"On the condition that she leave me behind and not have anything to do with me until I came of age."

"That's horrible." Her blue eyes darkened with compassion. "Rafiq, you must have been crushed."

"I was an infant and unaware of the circumstances." He shrugged. "I was raised by several attentive nurses and nannies. I wanted for very little."

"I don't believe that." She slipped the jewelry into his coat pocket. "Don't forget you have those. I can't believe she left you. Her child. I can't imagine any mother doing that."

Her combination of practicality and compassion delighted him. She was as he had imagined—without pretense. He could gaze into her eyes and see directly into her soul.

She leaned close and touched his face. "What she did was very wrong and I'll never forgive her."

"I'm sure she'll be disappointed."

Kiley smiled. "You know what I mean." Her smile faded. "Are you close now?"

"Not at all. We speak. I have lunch with her once or twice a year. She likes me to come to parties so she can show me off. Sometimes I agree to her request."

He had no opinion of his mother one way or the other. She had made her choice long ago. He had grown up without her and couldn't imagine a world in which she mattered to him.

"What of Eric?" he asked, capturing Kiley's hand in his and kissing the tips of her fingers. "You spoke?"

She nodded. "Not for long. Did you see us?"

"Yes. He was angry."

"I guess." She ducked her head. "When he said you were going to take advantage of me, I informed him that it was the other way around. I was using you for sex."

Rafiq laughed. "Good for you."

She looked at him. "I didn't feel anything. I tried, but there was nothing. A little anger that he was such a jerk and I'm still embarrassed by what I saw when he was doing it with that other woman, but that's it. Shouldn't

I be really upset by now? Shouldn't it all matter? What if I didn't love him?"

"Then not getting married is for the best."

"I know, but what does it say about me that I didn't realize I'd fallen out of love with him?"

"Sometimes we can't see what's right in front of us. You escaped. Be grateful."

"Oh, I am. He's the last man I would ever want to be with. What a loser."

Rafiq had grown tired of speaking of another man. He lightly licked her palm, then asked, "What are you wearing under your dress?"

The question stunned Kiley but didn't embarrass her. She recognized the light of passion flaring in Rafiq's eyes and couldn't wait to get close to the fire.

"A strapless bra and panties."

Nothing about his expression changed, but she felt the tension in his body. Her own answered with a slight quiver. He stood and held out his hand.

"Dance with me," he said.

She allowed him to pull her to her feet. There wasn't any music, but somehow that didn't seem necessary. The evening was perfect—something out of a movie, and she was the star.

He pulled her into his arms. She snuggled close and relaxed into the slow, swaying movements. She was aware of the night, the shadows in the corner, and the quiet. Her senses captured every detail of the moment— the scent of his body, the heat growing between them, the smooth fabric of his shirt, the way his cheek brushed against her temple. She wanted with an intensity that surprised her. He would be her first time, but somehow that thought no longer made her nervous. She welcomed his touch and his instruction.

He kissed her shoulder, then her neck. She turned her head so their mouths could meet. His firm lips pressed against her own. She parted for him, wanting him to take her, to tempt her until she was willing to do anything.

He swept inside and she tasted the wine and the man. As they kissed, she felt his hands on her back. They moved up and down stroking her from shoulder to hip. The rhythmic movement both lulled and aroused. When he tugged at her zipper, she knew he meant to undress her.

Anticipation swept through her. She was eager for the next lesson, eager to discover everything. Rafiq drew back and looked into her eyes.

"When you were with Eric," he said quietly, "did he ever make you climax?"

Talk about a mood breaker, Kiley thought as she blushed, then reached for the front of her dress to keep it from slipping. She cleared her throat, then murmured, "Not really."

Rafiq smiled. "I wanted to be sure."

"Yes, well, now you are."

He cupped her face in his hands. "I want to please you tonight. I want to show you the pleasure locked in your body. Will you allow me that?"

The intensity of his gaze took her breath away. His words made her want to follow him to the ends of the earth. Speaking seemed impossible, so she nodded.

He dropped his hands to hers and slowly drew them down to her sides. Gravity took over and her dress dropped to the floor.

She stood there, practically naked and painfully exposed. Time passed, and he didn't speak, didn't react at all. Just when she was about to duck for cover, he groaned low in his throat, bent down and gathered her in his arms, holding her against him.

"I want you," he said in a low growl. "All of you. I want to touch you and taste you and claim you." He stared at her, his expression possessive. "You will be mine."

The proclamation thrilled her, as much as his physically sweeping her off her feet. No one had ever been interested enough to want to claim her before. She wasn't exactly sure what he meant, but she was willing to go along with whatever he had in mind.

Rafiq made his way into her bedroom and gently placed her on the bed. Before she could worry about what to do next, he pulled her close and began to kiss her.

Long, slow, deep kisses. Kisses that left her breathless and shaken and touched her soul. She clung to him, holding on to hard muscles, straining to get closer, even as he moved his hands over her bare back.

She liked the feel of him touching her skin. He explored the length of her spine, then cupped her hip before moving to the top of her bare thigh. Goose bumps erupted.

He shifted her so that she stretched out on her back, with him looming over her. His lips turned up slightly, as if he were about to smile. She brushed her thumb against his mouth.

"You're very beautiful," he murmured. "Your skin is soft." He rested his hand on her belly. "I want you to relax and enjoy what I do to you. Tonight is just for play, so you can get used to me being close to you."

She wasn't exactly sure what he meant, although she

was fairly certain he meant they weren't going all the way. She had a moment of disappointment, then he began to unbutton his shirt and she found herself distracted by his broad chest.

She put her hands on him and explored the contours, the way flesh molded muscle and how those muscles tensed when she lightly brushed over them. He bent down and kissed her. She parted for him, even as she slid her hands around to stroke his back.

He explored her mouth with his tongue, then slipped away before she'd had all she wanted. But as his destination seemed just as interesting as kissing, she decided not to protest.

Even as her eyes fluttered closed, she felt him move down her neck, then the hollow between her breasts. He licked her there, then nibbled on the sensitive skin by the edge of her bra. He moved his hand from her stomach around to her side. She shifted slightly so he could reach behind her and unfasten the hooks.

Her breath caught in anticipation as he pulled away the bra. A puff of warm air was her only warning, then his mouth claimed her right breast in an openmouthed kiss that made her body clench and her hands reach for him.

She touched his shoulders, his back, then buried her fingers in his dark hair.

"Yes," she breathed.

He licked her nipple, then sucked it into his mouth. After circling the taut tip, he raised his head slightly and blew on it. The combination of damp and cold and heat made her want to beg. Need filled every cell in her body. She ached, she wanted and she had to make sure he understood he could never, ever stop.

He moved to her other breast, and on the first, re-placed his mouth with his hand. She arched her head and savored his caress. Between her legs, her panties grew damp as that most feminine place began to ache.

When he left her breasts, she cried out in protest. "I'm not done," she told him.

She felt him laugh against her stomach.

"Trust me on this."

He moved lower, pausing to lick her belly button. The sensation was both ticklish and erotic. A combination she'd never experienced before. Then he reached the edge of her panties.

Eric had never bothered touching her there more than a couple of times and always through clothes. She remembered once when she'd straddled his knee and had rocked against him until he'd pushed her away. Now the aching intensified as she wondered what Rafiq would do there.

But first he tugged on her panties, pulling them down her legs, then tossing them away. She had the sudden thought that she was actually naked before a man—not counting doctors—for the first time in her life. Eek!

She opened her eyes and found him looking at her.

"Lovely," he said with a smile. "Every part of you. I like this spot." He touched her ankle. "And this one." He traced a circle around her knee. "And here." He slid a single finger between her tightly closed thighs.

She planned to be embarrassed and protest and squirm, but that wily finger slipped between her curls, the folds of skin and found an amazing, responsive bundle of nerves on the very first try.

Her eyes closed, her legs fell open and she didn't care if he looked at her all day, as long as he kept touching her.

"You like that?" he asked.

"Uh-huh."

"Good."

He continued to rub and circle and explore. She found herself getting lost in the perfect sensations that radiated out from that one spot. Her body burned, her blood seemed to flow faster. She was tense and yet perfectly relaxed.

He moved onto the bed, then nudged her thighs farther apart. She obliged him, even drawing back her knees. She felt his shoulder brush her leg and before she knew what was happening, he claimed her with a kiss.

She knew what he was doing. She'd read about it, seen it in movies, even talked about it. But until that moment, until his tongue brushed over her most sensitive spot with the exact pressure and speed designed to drive her into madness, she hadn't actually understood it.

The sensations were too exquisite, too perfect. She moaned as he licked her, moving a little faster, as if urging her on. Her hips arched in a rhythm she couldn't control. She dug her heels into the bed and pushed toward him, silently begging for more, for all.

Muscles clenched, her body writhed, she tossed her head back and forth as she strained to reach for something she couldn't quite grasp. For some…

He slipped a finger inside and circled it around. The combination was too much, and she felt herself lifted up as her body shattered in a rush of pleasure she'd never experienced before. Hazily she recalled a friend saying that if she had to ask if she'd climaxed, then she hadn't.

Now her release swept through her with the subtlety

of a thunderbolt. It was perfect, her muscles contracting and releasing as Rafiq continued to gently touch her. On and on it went until at last it slowly faded and she found herself back where she'd started, only much more satisfied.

"So that's what all the fuss is about," she sighed when he'd stretched out next to her and pulled her close. "I like it."

He chuckled. "Good."

She snuggled close, liking the feel of his arms around her. "We're going to do that again, right?"

"Yes. As often as you'd like. Although not tonight. I don't want you to get sore."

She was kind of thinking she would endure a little soreness for an experience like that again.

"Is it always that good?" she asked.

"It can be."

"Huh." She raised herself up on her elbow and looked down at him. "So how does anyone get any work done? Why don't people just stay in bed and make love all the time?"

"As pleasurable as that sounds, we have responsibilities."

"I guess. But given the choice…"

He reached between her legs and rubbed her. "I suppose we should consider a second time, just so you have a point of comparison."

She collapsed back on the bed and gave herself over to the pleasure. "If you insist."

Fate conspired to keep them apart. Kiley was determined to be brave about the whole thing. After what had happened Friday night she knew she wasn't in a position to complain that Rafiq had a previous engagement over the weekend and then late meetings the following week. Still, now that she understood the possibilities, she wanted to explore them all.

Wednesday afternoon she sat in his office with a pad of paper, a pen and a list.

"It's your sister's birthday in two weeks," she said. "You need to send a present. I have a list here, if you'd like to choose one."

He raised his eyebrows. "I'm not qualified to decide. You may send what you like."

"You always say that. Don't you want to know what they're going to be thanking you for?"

"I have little contact with my half sisters. I'm sure they're delightful young women who know nothing of their half brother and do not consider themselves injured by the lack of contact."

"You're being cynical."

"It is one of my best features."

"Want to take a vote?"

"An impartial panel would agree with me," he told her.

"Not if it was made up of women."

He leaned back in his chair. "Is this your subtle way of issuing a complaint?"

"Not at all. I think it would be nice if you picked out your sister's present yourself."

"And yet I will not." His dark eyes flickered with something she couldn't read. "Anything else?"

She squirmed in her seat. "I haven't seen you all week."

"I know. My meetings have gone on later than I would like." He smiled. "I have missed you."

Not as much as she'd missed him, she thought. It was like not knowing she'd been starving, then being offered a fabulous meal, only to be told the buffet was now closed.

"Me, too."

"We will have more time this weekend."

Not as much as he thought. Her sister had just had a baby and Kiley wanted to go home for a couple of days. "Actually we—"

The phone in her office rang, cutting her off. She rose to answer it just as his phone rang. Later, she thought. She would tell him that she would be leaving town for the weekend.

"This is Kiley," she said as she picked up the phone.

"Hi, Kiley. My name is Marcy Dumont. We met at the fund-raiser last week. Do you remember?"

Kiley really didn't, but doubted that was the point. "Of course. How can I help you?"

Marcy laughed. "Actually, and this may sound a bit strange, I need you to talk to Rafiq."

"He's right here. You can speak with him yourself."

"I know I *could* but I think it would be better if you did. I work with a children's charity here on the Westside. We would very much like Rafiq to sponsor one of our events. I'd like to send you the information to look over. If you like what we're doing, you can talk to him about it."

It took Kiley a minute to figure out what was going on. "You think there's a better chance he'll say yes if I ask him?"

Marcy laughed again. "Are you kidding? We all saw the way he looked at you. He wouldn't refuse you anything. And it's for sick kids, Kiley. I wouldn't ask otherwise. I'm going to pop the information into the mail. My business card will be there. Check it out, then give me a call."

"But I—"

"Talk to you soon." Marcy hung up.

Kiley did the same, then stared at her phone. It wasn't that she minded helping sick children, she thought grimly. It was that she didn't like being manipulated. Her relationship with Rafiq was private. No one had the right to use that to influence either of them. She felt uncomfortable and unsure of what to do. If the cause had been anything else, she would have simply ignored the material. But sick children? She couldn't just turn her back.

"I need the quarterly reports," Rafiq said from the doorway between their offices.

"I'll get them right away."

He waited until she'd returned with the files, then took her hand. "What's wrong?"

"Nothing."

He stared at her. "Was that Eric on the phone?"

"What? No. He hasn't called."

Rafiq continued to study her. "We have an agreement of fidelity."

She smiled. "Trust me, I'm not about to forget it. Eric didn't call, hasn't called, isn't going to call. If he did, I wouldn't be interested. I swear."

He nodded once, as if satisfied, then returned to his office.

Chapter Seven

"I'm glad we're finally spending the evening together," Rafiq said Thursday night as he and Kiley were
shown to a corner table in the small Italian restaurant in
Santa Monica. He'd chosen to give up the view of the
ocean in favor of privacy.

"Me, too," she answered. "You've been busy."

"Unexpected meetings and out-of-town associates.
Fortunately, they are over now. There shouldn't be any
more interruptions."

She smiled at him and put her napkin in her lap. She
was beautiful in her low-cut blue dress. She would have
been more beautiful without it, but he was not about to
share her charms with the other patrons.

The waiter hovered until Rafiq requested the wine

list, then sent him away. But instead of glancing at the pages of available bottles, he stared at Kiley.

"You have something on your mind," he said.

She blinked. "Not really."

"I have felt it for the past day or so."

She shook her head, denying the charge, but he doubted her. Kiley had been forthcoming in the past, but she wasn't now. Did she worry that the topic would distress him? There was only one reason for that—she missed Eric.

He shouldn't be surprised. A few short weeks ago, she'd wanted to marry the man. She had told him she wanted revenge and he had believed her. Perhaps that had been a mistake. Was a woman's heart truly capable of revenge?

"The food here is excellent," he told her, knowing he would come back to the subject of her distraction later. "The chef is very popular. Would you like wine with dinner?"

"Yes, thank you. I'm going to let you pick because what I know about wine wouldn't impress anyone."

"Do you have a preference?"

"Not yucky."

He smiled. "I'll keep that in mind."

She opened her menu and studied the options. He did the same, then picked a wine. When they'd ordered, she leaned forward.

"My sister just had a baby. My mom called the night before last to tell me all about it. This is Heather's first. She's my baby sister. She'd always said she wanted complete natural childbirth. She's into organic everything. So when the time came, she refused to let them give her anything for the pain."

Kiley's mouth twitched slightly. "But Heather isn't very accommodating when she doesn't feel well. Apparently she was screaming so much, the other women in labor came into her room and begged her to take something. She was distracting them. My mom said it was pretty funny. Heather agreed and quieted down, and the baby was born. She had a girl."

Her expression turned wistful.

"You had planned to have children with Eric," he said.

"Three or four. He wanted to wait, but I was willing to get started right away. I always thought a big family like mine would be great. Sure it was messy and loud being one of three, but there was so much love."

"All girls?"

She grinned. "Does that horrify you? No possibility of heirs?"

"It isn't a concern for everyone."

"That's true. I think my dad likes being the only guy in the house. We all treat him very well."

"I think you will be a good mother."

She sighed. "Thank you. I know I'll try. I feel as if I could easily love a couple of dozen kids, but there is the reality of keeping track of everyone." She offered him the bread basket, then took a roll for herself.

"I keep thinking about how it's going to be," she said. "I want to have the house where all the neighborhood kids comes to play. I want to make Halloween costumes and bake and decorate for the holidays. I want a Christmas tree filled with ornaments made out of Popsicle sticks and a couple of dogs making trouble. A suburban fantasy."

"It sounds very nice."

"Oh, right. So speaks the prince."

"Do you think I'm not interested in a domestic situation?"

"I don't know. Are you?"

"I will marry and have children."

"That's right," she said. "We've discussed your need to find the proper woman at the princess store. How's that working out?"

Before he could tease her back, the waiter appeared with the wine. He opened the bottle, then poured them each a glass. When they were alone, Kiley leaned toward him.

"I have a question," she said in a low voice, staring at his shirtfront rather than his face.

"Yes?"

"Is it really just business that's kept us apart? Physically, I mean?"

He reached across the table and took her hand. "Are you concerned?"

"A little. Last weekend we, um, made some progress and since then, well, nothing. Did I do something wrong? I've been thinking about it and I wondered if maybe you thought I was being selfish. The whole thing was about me. I feel really bad about that. I just didn't think…" She bit her lower lip. "Pleasing the man in my life isn't something I'm used to."

Her combination of worry, concern and nervousness charmed him. He squeezed her fingers.

"You are the innocent in the relationship," he told her. "I don't expect you to be aware of my needs or responsible for them. Had I wished things to go differently, I would have told you."

"Okay. But it's been a week. Things were really hot and heavy before." She glanced around, as if making sure no one could hear them. "Are you unhappy with me? Do you want to change your mind about the whole mistress thing?"

If they'd been alone, he would have claimed her right at that moment. He was delighted that she missed their physical contact.

"You are the one I desire," he said, staring into her eyes. "Only you."

Her mouth parted, but she didn't speak. He felt her pulse quicken and heard her breathing increase.

"Wow," she whispered at last. "That's good."

"It's true."

"So you really have been busy? It's just that?"

"Mostly. Also, I thought we were moving a little quickly. I wanted to give you time to get used to our intimacy."

"Now? You take me to the pleasure planet, then pull back? It hardly seems fair."

He smiled. "Then we can change things. You only have to let me know. Or better yet, show me."

Her eyes widened. "As in, seduce you? I'm not sure I know how."

His body clenched at the thought. "You would figure it out." In truth, it wouldn't take much, but she didn't need to know that. Just sitting here with her, talking about making love, was enough to get him hard.

"Really?" She pulled free of his touch, clapped her hands together and shimmied in her seat. "I like that. I like the thought of bringing a big, powerful prince to his knees. Figuratively, of course."

"Of course. Maybe this weekend we can—"

"Hello, Kiley."

Rafiq glanced to his left and saw Eric standing next to their table. Annoyance destroyed his good mood.

Kiley jumped. "Eric! What are you doing here?"

Her surprise seemed genuine. As much as Rafiq wanted to grab the smaller man by the shirt and pummel him, he deliberately decided to wait and see what happened. If Kiley needed his help, he would step in—otherwise it would be better if she took care of Eric herself.

"I have to talk to you," Eric said, ignoring Rafiq. "Come outside."

"I'm not going anywhere with you. Go away."

Not the words of a woman mourning a relationship, Rafiq thought with relief.

"You're making a fool of yourself," Eric said, glaring at her. "Can't you see that?"

"The only fool here is you," she told him. "You didn't realize what you could lose. It's gone now and there's no getting it back. I'm sorry if that hurts, but..." She frowned. "*No.* I'm not sorry. I'm glad it hurts you. I hope it hurts a lot. You treated me terribly. I'm not interested in you or our past or anything you could say to me. My biggest regret is that I wasted three years of my life waiting to marry you. The bright spot is I found out the truth before the wedding."

Eric turned on Rafiq. "This is your fault. You seduced her. How long were you screwing her before all this happened?"

Rafiq started to rise, but Kiley put her hand over his. "I appreciate it," she said, "but I can handle this."

He nodded and sank back in his chair. He would let her be in charge…for now.

"Rafiq has nothing to do with it," she told Eric. "The only one who was unfaithful in our relationship is you. Of course, given how much you cheated, it makes sense that you would assume the worst about everyone else. But I'm not like that. I take my commitments seriously."

"So this just happened?" Eric asked, sounding incredulous. "I find that tough to believe."

She shrugged. "I don't care what you think. Your opinion doesn't matter to me. Not anymore. It's over between us and I'm relieved. I think it's sad I'm not in more pain. It makes me think I haven't loved you for a long time."

Eric pointed at Rafiq. "You replaced me with him? You're an idiot if you think it's going to last. You're caught up in his money and title, but that's not going anywhere. He'll never marry you. You're from different worlds. He thinks this is fun now, but he'll get tired of you and then toss you aside."

"Maybe," Kiley said calmly. "The difference is when Rafiq wants to end the relationship, he'll say it to my face. He'll be honorable. He won't cheat on me behind my back."

Eric reached for her. Rafiq grabbed his arm. "I wouldn't do that if I were you."

Eric jerked free and retreated a step. Rafiq let him.

"I'm not the only one who sneaks around, Kiley," Eric said. "What about you? Do your parents know about him? Do they know what you're doing? It's not as if you're willing to take him home this weekend to see Heather's new baby."

Kiley had been mad before, but now she was furious. She'd seen Rafiq grab Eric. From the look on Rafiq's face, he would be happy to beat up the other man. She was almost tempted to let him do it.

"How dare you?" she breathed. "You called my parents."

"Of course I did. I'm worried about you. They mentioned the baby and that you'd be coming to visit." Eric turned to Rafiq. "Didn't know that, did you? Kiley has a big family. I was always welcome there. They liked *me*. Think they'll say the same about you?"

Kiley wasn't sure what her family would say about Rafiq, and she wasn't planning to find out. In truth, now that Heather had had her first baby, Kiley wanted to go home for the weekend. She'd planned to tell Rafiq over dinner. She still would. She just hated how Eric made it sound as if she were keeping secrets.

Rafiq leaned back in his chair and regarded Eric. "Kiley was telling me about the baby when you interrupted. It is unfortunate you've finally realized what you lost, but the fault is yours. Kiley is gone and you have no one to blame but yourself."

Eric took a step toward him. "I oughta nail you."

Rafiq placed his napkin on the table and stood. He topped Eric by several inches and outweighed him by fifteen or twenty pounds of muscle.

"Do you think that's possible?" Rafiq asked with a casualness that belied his temper.

Kiley didn't know what to do. A part of her wouldn't mind if Rafiq beat the crap out of her ex-fiancé. But this was a public place and she didn't think Rafiq would appreciate the potential publicity.

Just then an older man hurried toward them. Two burly cooks and a big waiter accompanied him. He paused by the table and bowed his head.

"Prince Rafiq, I'm so sorry. I did not realize this man was bothering you. Please allow me to escort him outside." The man snapped his fingers, and the two cooks grabbed Eric.

"Hey, you can't do this," Eric said.

"It seems he can," Rafiq said as he sat down. "Know this. If you bother Kiley again, I will speak with the senior partners at your law firm. She has told you to stay away from her. It would be best for you and your career if you did just that."

Eric was hustled out of the restaurant before he could respond. Kiley felt the interested stares of the other diners.

"I'm sorry," she said, barely able to look at Rafiq. "I don't know how Eric found us or why he even bothered looking."

"Are you all right? Did it trouble you to see him?"

"It's embarrassing to have him make a fuss, and I hate that you had to get involved."

"I would have stepped in sooner, but I thought you would want to handle him."

"I did." She reached for her wine and took a sip. "I don't get it. He was so willing to ignore me for so long. Now that I'm gone, he's acting as if it's a big deal."

"Perhaps it is," Rafiq said. "He realizes what he lost."

"So what? I was an idiot for ever getting involved with him. What a weasel."

Rafiq nodded slowly. "There is a strength about you I didn't recognize at first. I admire that."

His compliment pleased her. "Thank you. I don't feel especially strong. Determined, maybe."

"Was Eric the reason you've been distracted for the past couple of days?"

He'd noticed? And here she thought she'd been keeping her worries to herself. Was she really bad at concealing things or was he more observant than most?

"No. It wasn't Eric. It's actually a couple of things. I didn't want to bring them up at work because I'm trying to keep our personal life out of that."

"Now I'm intrigued."

She drew in a deep breath. "A woman called. Marcy Dumont. I guess I met her at the fund-raiser, although I don't remember her specifically. There were so many introductions. Anyway, she wanted me to talk to you about sponsoring some event. It's for children."

She picked up her fork, then set it down. "It was so strange. I didn't know what to say to her and I felt really awkward. I mean, why come to me for money? She said I could influence you, which is crazy. I couldn't. But even if I could, I think it's wrong to impose on my personal life. She should have talked to you directly."

He was quiet for a long time. She knew he was reasonable enough that he wouldn't blame any of this on her, but she felt awkward about the whole thing.

"None of this is your fault," he said at last. "You're right. If the woman wanted me to sponsor an event, she should have contacted me. What did you tell her?"

"Nothing. She hung up before I could get my thoughts together. I've never had to deal with anything like this before. I didn't know how to handle the situation. Eric's right about that. We *are* from different worlds."

"Next time tell me," he said gently. "I will take care of things."

"I'm not helpless."

"I agree. But you're also not experienced in the nuances of my lifestyle. Your only responsibility is to me."

She couldn't help smiling. "That sounded very sheik-like and demanding. That my only responsibility is to you. As if you're the center of my world."

He raised his eyebrows. "I am Prince Rafiq of Lucia-Serrat. Of course I'm the center of your world."

She laughed, and her worry faded away. "Not on this planet, but it's a nice fantasy."

"You do not respect me."

"I respect you plenty, but I'm not a doormat. I'm an independent woman who chose you to be her lover."

As soon as she spoke the words, she clapped her hand over her mouth. "I did *not* say that aloud."

"You did." He picked up his wine. "I like this independent side of you. Tell me more."

"There's not all that much to say." Except for this one thing. She looked at him. "I have to go away this weekend."

His gaze sharpened slightly. "To visit your family?"

She shouldn't be surprised that he'd figured it out, but she was. "I want to see Heather and the new baby. It will just be for a couple of days. I'll fly out tomorrow and be back Sunday."

"You are welcome to be gone longer."

Not exactly the "I'll miss you" speech she'd been hoping for. "The weekend is plenty."

"Fine. I hope you enjoy yourself."

There was something about the way he said the words. Something that unsettled her.

"You're not mad, are you?" she asked.

"That you wish to visit your family? No. This is a very special time. You will want to be there."

Okay, that all *sounded* right, but it didn't feel right. She studied him, trying to figure out what was wrong. Did he seem to be sitting more stiffly? Was there a flicker of emotion in his eyes.

"I just…" She pressed her lips together. "What's wrong? Are you mad I'm leaving?"

"I assure you, I will survive without your company."

Ouch. "I know you will. Of course you will. You don't need me at all."

She stared at her plate and wondered where the conversation had gone wrong.

The waiter arrived and served their salads. Kiley picked up her fork, then put it down again. Suddenly she wasn't hungry.

"I'm sorry," Rafiq said quietly.

She looked at him and did her best not to show her astonishment. It had never occurred to her a real, live prince would ever apologize. "For what?"

"For hurting you." He shrugged. "I know your assumption is that I would not enjoy meeting your family. Perhaps you are uncomfortable with our relationship and who I am. It is better you go yourself. For my part, it has been a long time since I was reminded I am not like other men."

His words swirled around in her brain. Maybe she was crazy. Maybe she was delusional, but if she understood what he was saying then somehow *he'd* been hurt by her not wanting to take him with her.

"I'm not ashamed of our relationship," she told him.

"It is unconventional."

"I wouldn't exactly tell my mom about the terms of our agreement or that I was your mistress-in-training, but I would be comfortable introducing you. I thought you'd feel weird about going home with me. I thought you'd think it was dumb or boring. We're just regular people. No palaces, no fancy pedigrees. You're a prince."

"I am aware of my title."

She smiled. "I figured you were. Rafiq, you're used to who and what you are, but the rest of us aren't. My folks live in Sacramento in a tract home. We don't even have a second story."

"Are you concerned I'll judge your family and find them wanting?"

Interesting question. "No, I'm not," she said slowly, realizing it was true.

"Then what troubles you?"

When the truth came, it was both funny and sad. "I'm afraid you'll realize I'm not that special. That I'm just like everyone else."

"You are uniquely yourself."

"Does that mean you want to go with me this weekend?"

"I would like it very much."

"Then you should come along." Uh-oh. What exactly was she getting herself into?

Chapter Eight

They left for Sacramento Saturday morning, shortly before nine. The flight would be a little less than an hour, which meant there would be a whole day of family time. Usually the thought would have excited Kiley, but this morning it made her nervous.

Still, if she was going to bring Rafiq to visit her parents and whoever else might be hanging out there, it was very nice to travel in style.

"I've never been in a private plane before," she said as she rubbed her hand over the smooth, soft leather covering the seat. "It's very nice."

Rafiq sat across from her in an equally impressive seat. "There is a larger plane for longer trips."

"That's right. You have two planes."

He shrugged. "It is more convenient."

She had to agree with that. Instead of getting to the airport two hours early and dealing with long lines, they had driven onto a small airfield next to the Los Angeles International Airport. As soon as they had handed over their luggage and gone onboard, the pilot had prepared for takeoff. Who knew this type of travel even existed?

"You're going to make it hard to go back to discount flying," she said as the plane banked, then turned north.

"That was not my intent. I thought you would enjoy this plane."

She looked around at the luxuriously appointed cabin. "It's fabulous. Remind me to be rich in my next life."

"I will."

He unfastened his seat belt, leaned forward and unhooked hers. Then he pulled her across the narrow aisle onto his lap. When she'd settled onto his thighs and had looped an arm around his shoulder, he smiled.

"Much better," he said.

She snuggled closer. "What happened to taking things slowly?"

He put his hand on the back of her head and drew her down for his kiss. "I've been rethinking that plan."

"Good," she managed before he claimed her.

She pressed her hand to his cheek and let herself get lost in the sensual dance of lips and tongues. He explored her, then teased her by retreating. She followed, and he gently sucked on her tongue.

Need grew inside of her. She felt hot and hungry and her breasts ached.

He rested his hand on her thigh. She willed him to move higher, to touch her between her legs. Even through her jeans, the contact would bring her pleasure. But he didn't read her mind and she wasn't capable of asking. Not yet. But soon, she thought, wanting him with a passion that left her breathless.

She raised her head and sighed. "This is nice. I guess I should have seduced you this week, but I was really busy and time got away from me."

"I'm not sure how I feel about coming in second to your work."

"Specifically, it was a report my boss wanted."

He unfastened the buttons at the front of her shirt, then pressed his mouth to the swell of breast just above her bra. "Perhaps next time you should tell him no."

"I'd like to, but he's really demanding. You know the type."

"Regal," he said as he undid the front hook of her bra and pushed the cups aside.

He moved his hands to her hips and helped her straddle him. When she'd braced her hands on the back of the seat, he leaned in and took her nipple in his mouth. At the same time, he slipped his hand between her legs and began to rub her center. Perhaps he could read minds after all.

The combination of sensations was too much, she thought as she gave herself up to the gentle sucking at her breasts and the rhythmic teasing between her legs.

"Tell me the pilot isn't going to walk in on us," she said, her voice thick.

"Don't worry," Rafiq told her. "He won't. Relax."

As he spoke he moved his hands to the waistband of her jeans and unfastened the button there. She swayed back.

"You can't take my pants off," she said, shocked by the suggestion.

He smiled. "Why not? We have plenty of time."

"But we're in an airplane."

"I want to touch you. I want to feel your wetness and bury my fingers inside of you." The smile returned. "You don't have to enjoy it."

She was tempted by what he offered, but nervous about where they were.

"Just for a second," she said.

He chuckled, helped her to stand.

"I can't believe I'm doing this," she said as she slipped off her shoes, then tugged down her jeans. Her panties quickly followed.

Naked from the waist down, she straddled him again and braced herself on the seatback. He immediately went to work on her breasts, even as he made good on his word and slipped his finger inside of her.

She felt herself react instantly. Her muscles clenched around him as he moved in and out of her. At the same time, he used his thumb to rub against her swollen center. His mouth caressed her right breast and with his free hand, he went to work on the other one.

The man was talented, she thought hazily as she tensed in anticipation of her climax. Her eyes popped open. She couldn't! Not here. Not like that.

But everything felt too good. She didn't want him to stop.

"Just another minute," she whispered, her eyes drifting closed. "I'll count to sixty and then you'll have to—"

Her orgasm caught her unaware. One second she'd been determined to stay detached enough to stop, then next she lost herself in shuddering pleasure. She held in a cry of delight and rubbed herself against his hand.

When she was finished, she looked at him. "That was incredible."

"I would agree," he said, then kissed her.

She dropped her gaze to his crotch where she could clearly see his erection. "What about you? Don't you want to…you know?"

"Under other circumstances, I would say yes. But not here. Not your first time."

Soon, she thought as she stood and reached for her clothes.

"Just so you're clear, my family is completely normal," Kiley said as she pointed the way out of the airport.

Rafiq steered the rental car and wondered if she was nervous about him meeting her family or embarrassed about what had just happened on the plane.

He enjoyed giving her pleasure. In time he would take his own, but for now it was enough to please her.

"You have two sisters," he said. "Heather and…?"

"Ann. They're both married. And they'll be there, of course. Along with their husbands, in-laws, Ann's kids, some neighbors and Heather's new baby. A big crowd."

She sounded doubtful.

"It will be fun," he said firmly.

"I hope so. And I told you about the hotels, right? There's no really fancy one. At least, not that I could think of."

"I made us a reservation nearby."

She winced. "Okay, but if you hate it, you can go back to L.A. and I'll fly home on a commercial flight."

"Do you think me incapable of living without royal luxury for two days?"

"Not exactly." She bit her lower lips. "Okay, yes. I do." She hunched in her seat. "Don't hate me."

He laughed. "You're being far too dramatic. I will fit in perfectly, your family will adore me and I will adore them. Relax."

"I'm relaxed."

She looked tense enough to snap. "Yes, I can see that. What have you told them about me?"

"That you're my boss and we're friends. Not that we're dating or anything because this close to the wedding, that would be too weird to explain."

He doubted her family would think of him as just her friend, but he didn't say that to Kiley. She was already worried enough.

"I told you it was just a plain, one-story house, right?" she asked. "Nothing fancy."

He chuckled. "Relax. Everything will be fine."

Rafiq followed her directions and pulled up in front of a ranch-style home on a large lot. There were several cars parked in front. Kiley directly him to pull into the driveway, then sucked in a breath.

"Brace yourself," she said as she unfastened her seat belt.

Just then the front door burst open and several people spilled onto the front lawn.

There was an older couple he took to be her parents, a few small children, a woman in her twenties who looked a lot like Kiley and two men who were probably the husbands. He pushed open his door and got out.

Kiley climbed out of the rental car and hurried to her parents. They both hugged her, then her mother held her at arm's length.

"Are you all right?" the other woman asked. Rafiq assumed she was concerned about Kiley's reaction to the aborted wedding.

"I'm fine," Kiley said and hugged her again. "Great. Really." She squeezed her mother's arm. "Mom, Dad, this is my boss. Rafiq." She grinned. "Actually the official title is Prince Rafiq of Lucia-Serrat."

Her parents stared at him. Long experience had taught him that they weren't sure what was expected of them. He stepped forward and held out his hand to Kiley's father.

"A pleasure to meet you both," he said as they shook hands. He turned to her mother. "Mrs. Hendrick."

"Oh, dear. Just call me Jan. This is Jim. We're pretty informal around here." Jan smiled. "Are you really a prince?"

"I'm afraid so. It's true what they say—you can't pick your relatives. Please call me Rafiq."

They led him into the house where he was introduced to the rest of the family. In a matter of minutes he was in the den with the men, watching college football.

"We're Cal fans up here," Jim said from his place in the black leather recliner, next to the chintz-covered sofa. "Except for Bart there, who likes USC. You have a favorite team?"

"Oklahoma," Rafiq said easily. "This year they're going all the way. Last year's game against Florida showed everyone what they were capable of."

He glanced at Jim, who sat with his mouth open.

"I like football," Rafiq said with a grin.

"I guess you do. Huh. Never would have thought it." He glanced at the clock. "Jan won't let us have beers before noon on game day. Can't say that I blame her. But it's only during the season and it's nearly noon. Bart, you go on and get us some beers. Rafiq? Gonna join us?"

"Absolutely."

By late afternoon Rafiq had learned much more about the Hendrick family in general and Kiley in particular. He'd spent time with each of her sisters and her father. He'd heard about her disastrous appearance in a high school musical where she discovered she really couldn't sing, and had seen pictures of her in her cheerleading uniform. He'd watched her laugh with her sisters, play with the toddlers and melt over the newborn.

She was very much a part of her world and he could see she'd come by her desire to be a wife and mother honestly. Jan Hendrick clucked over everyone. She'd spent lunch filling plates, passing out sodas and mopping up after the little ones, and she'd done it with an easy grace that had impressed him.

He liked that they'd accepted him and even occasionally forgotten who he was. As he stood on the rear patio and admired the fading colors in the roses, he wondered what he would have been like if he'd been raised in a family like this instead of on Lucia-Serrat.

The back door opened. He turned and saw Jan step out.

"May I join you?" she asked.

"I would be delighted."

She sighed. "You have the nicest manners. I guess you get that, growing up as a prince and all."

"I had nannies and tutors who took etiquette very seriously."

"I can't even imagine." She leaned against the patio railing and looked at him. "I want to thank you for being there for Kiley. These past few weeks have been hard on her."

He studied the older woman's blond hair. There were only a few streaks of gray and, oddly enough, they added to her attractiveness. She had big blue eyes her daughter had inherited and a ready smile. She glowed with life and contentment, as if she'd gotten everything she'd ever wanted.

"Kiley has handled herself well," he said. "You should be proud of her."

"I am, as always. She's a good girl. Or should I say woman. She's all grown-up. And now she's had a big disappointment. I never took to Eric the way I took to the other girls' husbands, but I thought we'd learn to love him. Now, looking back, I can see there were signs, but none of us wanted to pay attention."

"Better she find out now rather than after the wedding."

"I agree." She studied him. "I can't tell you how much I want to ask you your intentions, but I won't. Kiley can handle herself. Still, I can't help worrying about her."

"She's a remarkable woman and I have great respect for her. I don't want to hurt her."

"Sometimes we don't get what we want. I'd like you to be careful with her heart. You're the kind of man a woman dreams about finding."

He grimaced. "Because I'm a prince?"

"I won't say that's not interesting, but it's not the main reason. There's something about you." She touched his arm. "Be kind to my little girl. That's all I can ask."

She walked inside the house. Rafiq watched her go. He almost wished he could have told her the truth. That she didn't have to worry. Kiley had come to him in order to get revenge and she had no interest in making their relationship about much more than that.

As he stood alone on the patio, he found himself wondering what it would be like if he were different. If he was the kind of man who believed in love and happily-ever-after. Then he would have to regret letting her go. But he didn't believe, and when the three months were up, he would walk away without looking back.

"My mother approves," Kiley said as they drove toward the hotel that evening.

Rafiq glanced at her. "I doubt that."

"It's true. She told me. She said you're everything a woman could want in a man." Her mother had also told her to be careful about getting her heart broken, but Kiley already knew that.

"I enjoyed meeting your family," he said. "They are good people."

"Thank you. I'd been afraid things would be awkward, but you fit right in." She glanced at him. "I had no idea you were a college football fan."

"I'm a man with many interests."

"Apparently." Right now she was one of them—but for how long?

Don't go there, she told herself. Don't think about the

future. There was only now. This night, this week, this month. Or three of them, to be precise. And then he would let her go.

When she'd asked about being his mistress, she'd been interested in revenge, nothing more. She hadn't thought about Rafiq as a person. Now she knew more of the man, and she liked him. She also admired him. Being in his company made her happy. She trusted him, laughed with him, wanted him. It was, she acknowledged, a recipe for emotional disaster.

She also knew that if she told him she was afraid of falling for him, he would break things off immediately. So she wouldn't say anything. She would live life to the fullest and deal with the consequences when their time was up. She would also abide by their agreement of an affair—nothing more.

She wanted to believe she mattered to Rafiq, and in some ways she was sure she did. But he was a prince, and the woman he chose to marry had serious implications. He wouldn't choose lightly, and he would never choose a regular woman from a completely normal middle-class American family. It just wasn't done.

There would be pain when the relationship ended, but she would survive. And in the surviving, she would learn and grow. Having been involved with Eric and then with Rafiq, she would know what to look for in a man and what to avoid. She would find the right partner, fall in love and start the family she'd always wanted. And for the rest of her life, she would have the memories of these three magic months.

They drove into the hotel parking lot and stopped by

the valet. As their luggage was unloaded by the bellman, Rafiq took her hand and led her inside.

He checked them in and followed the night manager to their room.

Tonight, she thought as the other man explained about the hotel amenities. They would be together tonight. She was tired of waiting, tired of being the student. She wanted to be his equal—a lover he found fascinating.

"Here is our presidential suite," the manager said as he opened one side of a double door.

Kiley looked at Rafiq. "I didn't book this."

"I know. I had my travel agent take care of it."

The room was lovely, with a view of the city, a spacious living room and two bedrooms. For her it was totally upscale, although she had a feeling that Rafiq normally traveled in more style.

Their luggage was brought up. He tipped the bellman, who left with the manager.

She crossed to the window and he followed. He stood behind her and wrapped his arms around her. She snuggled into his embrace.

"Thank you for staying over," she said.

"We had to. There's brunch tomorrow at your parents' house. I'm looking forward to it."

She smiled, then turned in his arms and touched a stain on his shirt. "I think the baby spit up on you."

"I am sure of it."

"You didn't mind being run over by toddlers or dragged into family arguments about where to go on vacation or the state of the roof."

"I enjoyed myself today. They are good people and they didn't have any expectations of me."

"A pleasant surprise?"

"You don't know how much."

She could imagine, though. The night of the fund-raiser had shown her that she wouldn't have enjoyed growing up in his world, always on display.

She studied his face, the handsome lines and masculine features. She touched his mouth and remembered how he'd touched her on the plane.

He smiled. "There are two bedrooms," he said. "Which would you prefer?"

She pointed to the master, with the large bed and marble bathroom. "That one."

"Then I'll take the other one."

"I don't think so."

His eyebrows rose.

She shrugged. "Unless it's really important to you, of course. I'm not going to force you to sleep with me."

"Kiley?"

"You said to let you know. So I am. I'm ready, Rafiq. I want us to make love tonight."

Chapter Nine

Her words made Rafiq hard in an instant. He ached to claim her right there, to strip off her clothes and bury himself inside of her. Control seemed unimportant in the face of his growing need.

But he held back. As much as he wanted to plunge himself inside of her, he wanted to make this good for her more. There would only ever be one first time for her. He would always be the first man to make her his. He wanted to make sure every moment of their love-making made her tremble with delight.

Without speaking, he took her hand and led her into the bedroom. Once there, he turned to her and pulled her close, then lowered his head so that he could claim her with a kiss.

He felt her instant surrender. She melted into him,

parting her lips and clinging to him. Her breasts pressed into his chest, her thighs brushed his.

He slipped his tongue into her mouth and tasted her sweet heat. She welcomed him, circling, rubbing, dancing. Each stroke, every brush, even the lightest touch of her fingers on his back inflamed him. Need pulsed in time with his heartbeat. He had never been one to simply take what was offered. He prided himself on reducing his bed partners to whimpering puddles of sexual satisfaction, but he had never *wanted* this much before.

It was as if the ancient blood of his heritage, of those long-gone desert warriors, now controlled him. He wanted to tear off her clothes and gaze upon her naked body. He wanted to move inside of her, filling her until they both cried out in ecstasy.

But she was a virgin and patience was required.

He forced the erotic images from his mind and gently stroked her back. He deepened the kiss, but made no other attempt to move things along. There would be plenty of time, he told himself.

She was the one to pull away and kiss his jaw. As she rubbed her body against his, she nibbled on his neck, then sucked his earlobe. His erection pulsed.

"You're going slow," she said, speaking into his ear.

"Yes. It's your first time."

"Don't."

He stiffened. "Don't what?"

"Don't go slow." She looked at him, and he saw the desire in her eyes. "I meant what I said. I'm ready. Touch me."

As she spoke, she unfastened the button on her jeans. He accepted the invitation and slid down the zipper, then eased his hand between her panties and her soft, warm skin.

Then he swore. She was hot, wet and already swollen. He rubbed the engorged center of her pleasure and made her moan. He eased a finger inside of her, and her hips arched toward him. He withdrew and she whimpered.

It was too much, he thought, battling animal urges. He could have held back if she'd been cautious or afraid or hesitant. He could have waited longer if she'd needed more time. But her blatant invitation was more than he could resist. More than he should have to.

He dragged her to him and kissed her again. But this time he claimed her as his. As he entered her mouth, he began unfastening the buttons on her blouse.

She reached for his shirt, but her inexperience slowed her down. He had her blouse off and her bra open before she'd managed two buttons. He broke the kiss and stepped back.

"Perhaps I should undress myself," he said as he finished unfastening his shirt, then tossed it aside.

"I'd like that."

She shrugged out of her bra and toed out of her shoes, then moved back into his embrace. Now her bare breasts rested on his skin. He could feel her tight nipples brushing against him. They groaned together.

He cupped both her breasts and caressed her with his fingers. As she dropped her head back and closed her eyes, he nudged her toward the bed.

Kiley felt the mattress behind her and waited for the flash of fear. There wasn't any. Just a building need that made her want to hurry things along. Her blood raced with an urgency that made it impossible to catch her breath. More. She wanted more. She wanted all of it.

She sank onto the bed, pulling Rafiq down beside her. He wrapped his arms around her and rolled, drawing her across him until they were both stretched out on the sheets. Even as he kissed her, he touched her breasts, rubbing, teasing, making her ache and need.

When his hand moved lower to her already-open jeans, she grabbed for the denim and pushed. Jeans and panties slid down her thighs until she was able to kick them and her socks off. He settled his hand between her legs and began to explore all of her.

She parted for him, knowing what would happen and more than ready to experience pleasure again. But this time was to be for both of them, so as he touched her, she reached for him.

He was hard. She felt the length of him through his slacks. Even as he circled around her and rubbed, she matched the movements on his erection.

After a minute or two he pulled back and looked at her. "You're distracting me."

"Really?" The thought if it made her smile.

"More than you know."

"Then let's do more."

He laughed and sat up. After taking off his shoes and socks, he stood and quickly removed his slacks and briefs. Then he was naked, and she could see all of him.

He was lean and muscled and very much aroused. When he joined her on the bed, she reached for him.

"I want to touch you," she said.

"I have something better in mind."

He knelt between her thighs. As she watched, he

gently parted her, then slowly began to push inside. At the same time, he rubbed that center spot, making it difficult for her to think about anything but the way he made her feel.

Still, even as her body tensed in anticipation of her release, she felt him filling her. The stretching was unfamiliar and a little uncomfortable. She stiffened slightly and he stopped.

"Does that hurt you?" he asked as he lightly caressed her breasts.

"Not really. It's just strange." She fought the need to close her eyes as his fingers worked their magic. "My doctor told me that I'm not going to bleed or anything. There's no physical proof." Ack! Talk about embarrassing. "You know what I mean."

"I do. Does this feel good?"

He lightly squeezed her nipples between thumb and forefinger.

"Oh, yeah. That works."

He moved his right hand between her legs. "And this?"

He began the rubbing again. Instantly she felt herself spiraling toward her release.

"Good," she gasped. "Really good."

"Then let me pleasure you."

He spoke softly, not the least bit commandlike, yet she found herself wanting to obey. He rubbed faster and faster, pressing a tiny bit harder, arousing her until release became inevitable. She felt him moving deeper inside of her but was more caught up in the rising tension and the way his fingers took her to the edge and then pushed her over.

Her climax engulfed her. She got lost in the waves of pleasure. He kept touching her. She rocked her hips,

The Silhouette Reader Service™ — Here's how it works:

Accepting your 2 free books and gift places you under no obligation to buy anything. You may keep the books and gift and return the shipping statement marked "cancel." If you do not cancel, about a month later we'll send you 6 additional books and bill you just $4.24 each in the U.S., or $4.99 each in Canada, plus 25¢ shipping & handling per book and applicable taxes if any.* That's the complete price and — compared to cover prices of $4.99 each in the U.S. and $5.99 each in Canada — it's quite a bargain! You may cancel at any time, but if you choose to continue, every month we'll send you 6 more books, which you may either purchase at the discount price or return to us and cancel your subscription.

*Terms and prices subject to change without notice. Sales tax applicable in N.Y. Canadian residents will be charged applicable provincial taxes and GST. Credit or debit balances in a customer's account(s) may be offset by any other outstanding balance owed by or to the customer.

If offer card is missing write to: Silhouette Reader Service, 3010 Walden Ave., P.O. Box 1867, Buffalo NY 14240-1867

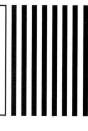

NO POSTAGE
NECESSARY
IF MAILED
IN THE
UNITED STATES

BUSINESS REPLY MAIL
FIRST-CLASS MAIL   PERMIT NO. 717-003   BUFFALO, NY

POSTAGE WILL BE PAID BY ADDRESSEE

SILHOUETTE READER SERVICE
3010 WALDEN AVE
PO BOX 1867
BUFFALO NY 14240-9952

GET FREE BOOKS and a FREE GIFT WHEN YOU PLAY THE...

Lucky 7

Just scratch off the silver box with a coin. Then check below to see the gifts you get!

SLOT MACHINE GAME!

YES!

I have scratched off the silver box. Please send me the 2 free Silhouette Special Edition® books and gift for which I qualify. I understand I am under no obligation to purchase any books, as explained on the back of this card.

335 SDL D73E   **235 SDL EE25**

FIRST NAME

LAST NAME

ADDRESS

APT.#

CITY

STATE/PROV.

ZIP/POSTAL CODE

7	7	7	**Worth TWO FREE BOOKS plus a BONUS Mystery Gift!**
🍒	🍒	🍒	**Worth TWO FREE BOOKS!**
♣	♣	♣	**Worth ONE FREE BOOK!**
🔔	🔔	🍒	**TRY AGAIN!**

www.eHarlequin.com

(S-SE-12/05)

DETACH AND MAIL CARD TODAY!

liking the sense of fullness as she came. Rocked a little faster until she realized he was moving, too. Moving inside of her.

Her eyes popped open. He was over her, his arms supporting his weight as he slowly moved in and out of her. She could see the tension in his face, the need in his eyes as he watched her.

"We're making love," she whispered.

"So we are."

"I like it."

"Good."

He moved a little faster. She spread her legs more, inviting him to go deeper. As he did so, she felt a hint of anticipation, a flutter of wanting. This had possibilities, as well.

But that was for next time. Now she simply wanted him to experience what she had.

"Come for me," she whispered.

He smiled. "As you wish."

He closed his eyes and pushed into her twice more before stiffening, then groaning her name.

Rafiq poured more champagne into Kiley's glass. "Are you still hungry?" he asked.

She looked at the demolished plate that had originally held a burger and fries, along with the empty bowl of what had been ice cream.

"Nope. I'm completely full." She sipped the bubbly liquid and grinned. "I've never had champagne with a hamburger before."

"What do you think of the combination?"

"I like it."

They sat next to each other on the comfortable sofa in the suite's living room. She pulled her robe more securely around her and tucked her bare feet under Rafiq's thigh.

It was done. She'd officially changed her status to nonvirgin, and the entire event had been spectacular.

"You look happy," he said as he rubbed her bare calf.

"I am. Thank you for tonight."

"My pleasure, and I mean that most sincerely."

She leaned against the sofa and smiled at him. "This has been a good day. One of my best ever. You made my first time perfect."

"I wanted to."

She believed him. She knew that he'd been concerned about her while they'd made love. She liked that about him, along with other things.

Who was this man who made love with her so wonderfully? How could she have worked for him for two years and never noticed his goodness and humor and how incredibly sexy he was?

"You don't go back to Lucia-Serrat very often," she said.

He looked at her. "An interesting change in subject."

"I was thinking that you've been little more than a boss to me until very recently. I never allowed myself to see the actual man inside the suit. Now I have and it changes things."

He nodded. "I don't go back to the island much. In time it will be important to me to live there permanently. But not yet. My father runs the country well. He is busy with that and with his wife and family."

Kiley tried to remember all she knew about Lucia-Serrat and its ruler. "His wife is American, isn't she?"

"Yes. Phoebe grew up mostly in Florida. They met when she was on vacation. They fell in love very quickly and have been married nearly twelve years. They have two daughters."

"I know. The half sisters you refuse to shop for. You're better about your brothers."

"That's because they're boys and I know what they want."

"Do you stay away to give them a chance to be a family?" she asked.

He shrugged. "In part. I would be expected to move into the prince's residence. While the girls are so young, it is better that they have their father's attention."

She snuggled close and rested her head on his shoulder. "Tell me about the island."

"It's very beautiful. There are beaches and a rain forest. One of the world's largest banyan trees is there. And, of course, the famous Lucia-Serrat meerkats."

"I love meerkats."

"Most women do."

"They look like little bandits. So cute. Do you miss your home?"

"Sometimes."

And yet he stayed away because it was the right thing to do. Talk about a tough act to follow. He was going to make falling in love with someone else a bit of a challenge.

She raised her head and sipped her champagne. "Do you know who you're going to marry?"

He stiffened slightly. "Why do you ask?"

"Don't panic," she said with a grin. "I'm not hinting. I'm asking. You're going to have to marry and have heirs. Do you know who it is? Have you picked out some innocent schoolgirl who will be raised in proper princess fashion?"

"Not yet. I may choose as I like or have my father arrange a match."

"That will never happen," she told him. "You're too stubborn to let someone else pick your wife. You might want to stay away from Carmen, though. She had quite the temper."

"I remember."

The nature of their conversation surprised Rafiq. He braced himself for the not-so-subtle hints indicating that Kiley would make the perfect wife, but they never came. Now that he thought about it, she had never mentioned extending their affair or talked about the future at all.

"You need someone tall," she said. "A lot taller than me."

"Why?"

She sighed. "Because, she'll look better in her clothes and therefore in all the pictures. There's a reason fashion models are so tall. Make sure she's smart and funny. You'd hate it if she was dull. But not too skinny. Look for childbearing hips."

"I find it disconcerting to discuss my future wife with my current mistress."

She looked surprised. "But we've seen each other naked. You deflowered me. I wouldn't have thought there were any topics off-limits. I guess I didn't know you were so sensitive."

"I'm not *sensitive*," he said with a growl.

She patted his arm. "Of course. My prince, a delicate flower. Who would have known?"

He took her glass and set it on the coffee table next to his own. He then grabbed her and pressed her back into the sofa.

"You dare to defy me?" he asked in mock anger.

"Pretty much every chance I get. Is that a problem?"

Her hair was mussed, her eyes the color of midnight velvet. His stubble had rubbed a raw spot on her chin, and the robe she wore was two or three sizes too large. She was possibly the most beautiful woman he'd ever seen.

"You are mine now," he told her. "I have been your first and you will always remember that."

"I know." She smiled and pressed her fingers to his mouth. "I guess neither of us is going to forget, huh?"

He hadn't considered that. Not forgetting. But she was right. Kiley would be with him, always.

"Come live with me," he said, speaking almost before the thought formed.

She blinked. "What? You mean move in with you?"

He understood her surprise. He'd never asked a woman to do that before. He hadn't felt the need to spend that much time with one of them before. But Kiley was different. He wanted her in his bed every night. He wanted to see her in the morning and late in the evening. He wanted her there when he returned home from work.

"Until our time is up," he told her. "Come live with me."

She stared at him, but he had no idea what she was thinking.

"Are you offended?" he asked.

"No. Of course not. A little shocked, maybe. I didn't expect you to ask. What if you get tired of me?"

"I won't." He couldn't imagine it.

She nodded slowly. "I'd need to keep my apartment.

I don't want to have to move my stuff into storage for three months and then move it back. I guess I could temporarily forward my mail. It's not like I have a dog or anything to worry about."

Always practical, he thought with a smile.

"Is that a yes?" he asked.

"It is. If you'd like me to, I'll move in."

"Good."

He bent down and kissed her. As he pressed his mouth to hers, he tugged at the robe until it pulled open, exposing her naked body to his touch.

She reached one arm around him and pushed the other between them.

"Two can play at that game," she whispered as she reached for him.

He was already hard and he relished the feel of her hand on his erection.

"I want to please you," she said.

He heard the hesitation in her voice. "You're sore."

"A little. So I was thinking about all the really interesting stuff you did to me. Could I do that to you?"

His interest quickened. "If you would like to."

Her answer was to push him until he was seated on the sofa. She slid onto the floor and moved between his knees. After taking him in her hands, she licked the tip of his arousal and then smiled.

"Tell me what to do."

Chapter Ten

Kiley walked through her apartment one last time before heading out to Rafiq's place. It was sort of sad to think she'd lived here for three years and had never done anything to make the place her own. Sure, she'd hung pictures and she'd sewn curtains for the eating nook by the kitchen, but she'd never checked with the manager about painting or bought any furniture she really loved. She'd decorated in early hand-me-down because she'd always planned to buy real furniture after she and Eric were married.

How much of her life had been on hold for those three years? How many things had she put off, waiting for the day she would get married and her life would change forever? Since she'd always wanted to be a wife and mother, she'd allowed that desire to reduce the rest of her life to a giant waiting game. In the end, she'd lost her dream and Eric—although that was turning out to be much less of a loss than she'd realized—and the time.

Where would she be if she hadn't expected to marry Eric and become a wife and mother? Although she loved working for Rafiq, in truth she would never have gone looking for a job she considered temporary. She would have looked until she found something that challenged her. Something that made her grow and gave her room for advancement. She would have looked for a career.

Talk about being foolish, she thought sadly as she picked up a picture of her family and tucked it in her tote bag. She'd given up too much for a man who wasn't worth it.

So what was she going to do now? What would she do differently? What changes did she want in her life?

Kiley stood in the center of her living room and turned in a slow circle. When her affair with Rafiq was over, she would start looking for another job. In truth, now that they were lovers, she knew she could never go back to being just his secretary. She couldn't stand to take calls from other women, knowing he was doing to them what he'd done to her. She wouldn't want to make reservations, buy gifts, watching from the fringes.

But expecting him to want to continue things past the three months was just plain crazy. He was a foreign prince and she was just some middle-class American girl. Sure, she was smart and funny and had a lot to offer. But a prince? On what planet?

No, this time she was going to keep her eyes open. This time she wasn't going to be a foolish dreamer. For the next two-plus months she was going to experience a world she knew very little about—everything from drinking champagne while eating a hamburger to living in a stunning home in Malibu. When the time was up, she would return to her regular world and build a life she could be proud of. There wouldn't be any looking back.

That decided, she locked the front door and walked to her car. As she started the engine, she thought about working out a plan with her parents. One in which she paid them back over time so she could buy a condo and have a place of her own. Maybe she would even get a dog.

But in the meantime she needed to get to Malibu. She wanted to see Rafiq, hold him and have him hold her. She wanted to see his smile and make love.

Thirty minutes later she drove down his driveway and stopped in front of the garage. As she stepped out, she looked at her aging but sensible car and started to laugh.

"What's so funny?" Rafiq asked as he walked out of the house toward her.

She grinned. "My car. It's not exactly fitting in with the neighborhood. Quick, get me a remote control for the garage door so I can hide it. Otherwise you'll get complaints from the neighbors."

He crossed to her and pulled her close. "Do you think I care what they think?"

"Not even a little. But it *is* important to build relationships in the community."

"Always the middle child," he said as he brushed his mouth against hers.

She let herself relax against him, enjoying the feel of his hard body so close to her own. She parted her lips and he swept inside. At the first brush of his tongue, tingles raced through her and made her toes curl. Funny how every time he touched her, she only wanted him more.

Trouble, she knew, even as she held on tight. At the end of this, he would walk away and look for his next conquest, and she…well, she wasn't sure what she would do. She had a feeling that getting over Rafiq was going to be more difficult than getting over Eric. Perhaps a smarter woman would have been able to resist Rafiq's considerable charms. Or a more-experienced one. But she didn't know how and now it was too late.

A once-in-a-lifetime event, she reminded herself. That's what this was. If the price was pain at the end, then so be it. She was strong and she would recover.

"Come inside," he said, stepping back and taking her hand in his.

She smiled. "Are you about to use me for sex, because if that's the case, I have to tell you, I won't protest."

He led her to the front door, then waited for her to step inside.

"I had wondered if you being so innocent would make things more difficult," he said.

She stared through to the living room where the ocean stretched out before her. It was as if she could see to the ends of the earth.

She turned back to him. "What was your concern? That I might be shy and afraid of intimacy?"

"It crossed my mind."

"I guess." She shrugged. "To be honest, I have a lot of time to make up for. I guess you'll just get stuck with that."

"I'll do my best to survive."

"How manly of you."

He wrapped his arm around her. "Are you hungry? Would you like something to eat?"

"Are you offering to cook?"

He moved her toward the kitchen. "No, but I have a very efficient housekeeper who keeps my refrigerator filled with items that need only be heated."

They walked into the large, open kitchen. Kiley crossed to the smooth granite countertops and ran her hands against the cool surface. She stared at the six-burner stove, the warming drawer and did her best to hold in a moan.

"Will she mind if I cook in here?" she asked.

"Sana would be happy to share."

Kiley looked at him. "Are you sure? Women can be very possessive about their kitchens."

"Sana would be delighted if I dated someone who knew how to make toast, let alone an entire meal. I assure you, she will not be offended."

Kiley had to admit she couldn't imagine the very beautiful, albeit short-tempered, Carmen knowing her way around much more than an espresso machine or an ice bucket.

"I'll have to come up with a menu," she said. "Then I'll dazzle you."

"You already do."

His words made her whole body sigh.

"Come," he said, holding out his hand. "I know I gave you a tour the first time you were here, but I suspect you were too nervous to remember very much. There is also the matter of where you will be sleeping."

"Didn't we already have this conversation at the hotel?" she asked, walking to him and letting him capture her fingers.

"That was for a single night. This is for more than two months." His dark gaze studied her face. "You have made many changes in the past few weeks. I don't want you to feel you're being pushed into something you're not ready for."

He was sweet. Funny how she'd never realized that before. Sweet and kind and handsome and charming. Talk about a winner.

She stepped close enough for their bodies to touch. With her free hand, she rubbed his chest.

"I'm here for the sex," she said in a low voice. "I want to be perfectly clear about that. Being in different rooms is going to make that difficult. Unless we do it on the phone, and, honestly, I'm not ready for that."

His reply was a kiss that took her breath away. He claimed her passionately, wrapping his arms around her and holding her as if he would never let her go.

"Then we will share a room," he said when they both came up for air.

She had a sudden thought and winced. "Oh, no. Were you trying to tell me that *you* wanted separate rooms?"

He rubbed against her, pushing his erection into her belly and turning her thigh muscles to mush.

"What do you think?" he asked.

She smiled. "I would say you've got yourself a roommate."

Sunlight and the sound of running water woke Rafiq. He'd forgotten to set the alarm and had slept later than usual. Perhaps because he'd gone to sleep so early this morning.

He stretched, then placed his hands behind his head

and stared up at the ceiling. It *had* been a late night. Every time he'd tried to roll over and go to sleep, he would feel Kiley in the bed. She would move or sigh or even just breathe and then he would want her again. Wanting her, he would reach for her. She always welcomed his touch, joining him eagerly in whatever game he wished to play.

While he knew intellectually that she had been a virgin, he would never have guessed how quickly and easily she would discover the pleasures of making love. He barely had to touch her to make her swollen and ready. She raced toward her climax with an eagerness that only made him want to please her more.

The shower turned off. Instantly he pictured her wet and naked. His erection was instant, but he held back. No doubt she was already sore from their previous night. Better to give her a few hours' rest before claiming her again.

He thought about his meetings planned for the day and the weekly teleconference with the parliament leader back on Lucia-Serrat. About twenty minutes later, Kiley opened the bathroom door and stepped into the bedroom.

She was dressed in her usual skirt and blouse. Her short, spiky hair was slightly damp, her makeup fresh. Tiny gold studs decorated her earlobes. She looked prim and proper and it was all he could do not to rip the clothes from her body and take her right there.

"Morning," she said with a shy smile.

Rafiq smiled back. "How are you feeling?"

"God. This is kind of a first for me. A sleep-over. Although, we did at the hotel, so I guess not technically. Maybe it's the whole workday thing. Plus, I'm tired. We didn't get much sleep either night. Not that I'm complaining. So, how are you?"

"Well. Did you want to rethink our living arrangement?"

"What? No. Of course not. I like being here."

"But you are not comfortable."

"I will be. Just give me some time. It's not every day a girl signs up to be the love slave of a prince. Ohh, maybe they'll make a cable movie about my life. What do you think?"

That she charmed him. That he wanted her in more than his bed, he wanted her in his life.

The realization surprised him, and not in a pleasant way. He knew about commitments, what they meant and what happened when people grew tired of them. He knew that love didn't exist, and whatever feelings people claimed in the heat of the moment faded over time.

"Go eat breakfast," he said as he sat up. "I will join you shortly."

She smiled and left the bedroom while he considered why Kiley had the ability to make him wish that things were different, that marriages could be happy and long lasting.

Perhaps it was her family, he thought. They embodied what most people aspired to. But how much of it was real? Did Kiley's sisters' husbands really stay faithful to their wives? Did they love them through childbirth and teething and job losses?

He doubted it. In his world, love was a convenient word used to manipulate. His father had claimed to love him and then had disappeared for months on end. His mother had claimed she hadn't wanted to leave him all those years ago. It wasn't her fault—the money was too good. And the women who moved in and out of his life—how many of them claimed to love him? And when it was over, how quickly did they take up with someone else?

Even Kiley, who was soft-hearted and inherently honest, had forgotten about her fiancé quickly enough. Although, in that case, he was willing to believe she hadn't loved the other man in some time.

No, this was better, he told himself. Taking for the moment. Better to have her leave while he could still think of her fondly than to have things end badly with recriminations on both sides.

He showered and dressed quickly, then found Kiley in the kitchen, eating breakfast and chatting with Sana, his housekeeper.

The tiny, dark-haired woman nodded approvingly as he walked in.

"This one appreciates my cooking," she said, pointing at Kiley's plate of pancakes and fresh fruit. "Not like the others who only want coffee. As if their skinny hips would appeal to any man."

"You've made a friend," he told Kiley, accepting the cup of coffee Sana handed him.

"I love her cooking, and she's telling me all of your secrets. What's not to like?"

He raised his eyebrows, but his housekeeper only shrugged. "I am an old woman. You won't throw me out, so I can do what I like, hey?"

Kiley grinned. "And she likes to talk."

"I have no secrets," he said, refusing to be intimated by a woman older than his mother.

"So you would like to think. What about the one who threw things? You wouldn't want me talking about her, would you? Or the one who sunbathed naked out there on the deck for all the world to see. The teenage boys in the neighborhood would stand on the sand with their binoculars."

Kiley wrinkled her nose. "That's kinda tacky, Rafiq. I'm surprised at you."

He narrowed his gaze. "We should change the subject."

"Oh, look," Kiley said with a grin. "He's getting imperious. I love it when that happens."

"You're not going to be like this at the office, are you?" he asked, already knowing the answer.

"Oh, please. I'll be perfectly professional." She waited until Sana walked to the far end of the kitchen, then looked him in the eye. "No one but you will know I'm not wearing any underwear."

Heat boiled his blood. He glanced down at her skirt. "You're kidding, right?"

She picked up her plate and carried it to the sink. "I guess you're going to have to wait until tonight to find out."

She returned to the island and picked up her handbag. "Thanks, Sana. That was fabulous. And what you suggested for dinner sounds perfect." She turned to Rafiq. "By, honey. See you at the office."

He followed her to the garage. "Not so fast."

She blinked at him. "Are you going to attack me right here in the hallway? I wouldn't want to get on Sana's bad side and have her think *I'm* tacky."

"You're more concerned about my housekeeper's feelings than what I want?"

"Pretty much."

She opened the door to the garage, stepped into the large, four-car structure and came to a complete stop. Rafiq put his hands on her shoulders and squeezed.

"What do you think?" he asked.

Kiley didn't know what *to* think. She'd been having fun, enjoying her morning, her breakfast, the possibility of a new friend and feeling at one with the universe. She liked that she felt confident enough to tease Rafiq about not wearing underwear, even though she was, and that he wanted her. She liked knowing what would happen when they got home that evening. She'd been quiet, shy and uncertain a few weeks ago, and today she was a different woman. Or she had been until five seconds ago.

"Kiley?"

She stared at the shiny red convertible parked next to her old sedan. The big white bow and ribbon gave her an idea it was a present. For her.

"You're giving me a car?" she asked, not sure what to think.

"Yes. Do you like it?"

It was gorgeous. Sporty and sleek, no doubt really fast.

"If you prefer a different color, we can exchange it."

Sure, she thought, not quite able to catch her breath. Just like socks.

"I, ah…"

"You don't like it," he said, sounding disappointed.

"No, I'm just surprised. No one's ever bought me a car before."

"But Eric gave you gifts."

"Not a car."

He turned her until she faced him. "Is it the money?"

"Well, yeah."

He smiled. "I am Prince Rafiq of Lucia-Serrat. Do you think this was any more financially significant to me than a book would be to one of your sisters?"

"No." She could do math. This wasn't even a drop in the bucket for him. It was barely a molecule of water. But… "It's a car."

He took her hand and brought it to his mouth, where he pressed his mouth to her palm. "You delight me in more ways than I can explain. It would give me great pleasure if you would accept this small token of my admiration for you."

She looked at the car, then at him. "What do you give when you want to offer a big token of admiration?"

"A castle."

She smiled. "I understand your point, but this is really strange for me."

"Would you rather have something else?"

Time, she thought. She would rather have more time with him. But to say that would break the rules, and she was determined to abide by them.

"I don't want anything except what I already have," she said. "You."

"But what about what I want? Take the car. When we are finished, you may sell it if you prefer. It is yours."

"I'll drive it while I'm here, but when it's over, I'm leaving it behind," she said.

"I will convince you otherwise."

"Not a chance," she told him. "I have a will of iron. You just haven't seen it yet."

She could tell he didn't believe her, but that wasn't important right now. Instead she focused on the kiss he gave her, then settled into her sassy red convertible and reminded herself this was all about living for the moment.

Chapter Eleven

"No," Kiley said later, her blue eyes wide with something that looked very close to terror.

Rafiq feigned surprised. "You are refusing me?"

"That's generally what no means. Although if used with another word such as 'no kidding,' it sometimes means something else entirely."

"I'm very familiar with the English language." He shook his head. "We are barely a month into our relationship and already you ignore my modest wishes."

She stood in the center of the bedroom, a silk robe clinging to her curves. Her hair was wet, her face scrubbed clean of any makeup. She shouldn't have aroused him, and yet she did. He was very familiar with the rush of desire he experienced whenever she was around.

"I'm not ignoring your wishes," she told him. "I'll take care of all your wishes, just not this one."

"It is a simple matter," he said.

She raised her arms and tightened her hands as if she wished to strangle him.

"It's entertaining. You never said anything about entertaining. I don't entertain. Oh, sure, I can have a few friends over for casual party or a football game or something. But not like this. We're talking about the American ambassador to Lucia-Serrat. That's not casual. That's really formal. I'm living here. I'm your mistress. What will he think? What will his wife think?"

Rafiq held in a smile. "Actually, the new American ambassador to my country *is* a woman."

Kiley made a half-growling, half-laughing noise low in her throat, turned and collapsed facefirst on the bed. "That would be my point. I don't even know who the new ambassador is. I can't be responsible for entertaining. You do it. Have a great time. Save me some leftovers."

"Kiley, it's not so bad."

She rolled to her side and glared at him. "You didn't make Carmen entertain any ambassadors."

"She was not up to the task."

"Neither am I. What are we supposed to talk about? My idea of staying on top of current events is whatever I get on the local news radio station during my drive to work. I don't know social-economic policies or what's happening in Bosnia. I don't even know if I could find Bosnia on a map."

He frowned. "Why would we discuss Bosnia?"

"I don't know. It could come up. Or another country. And then what? I'll stand there with my mouth open, looking really fishlike. It's not a plan for success. You have the party and tell me all about it."

"Social events are part of the deal," he said.

She shifted onto her back and covered her eyes with her forearm. "You never said I had to entertain."

"Would you have refused me if I had?"

"Maybe." There was a pause, then she sighed. "No. I wouldn't have. But this is really, really a mistake." She sat up and looked at him. "I'll do anything if you don't make me give a party."

He walked to the bed and took her hand. After pulling her to her feet, he lightly kissed her. "As appealing as your offer is, I must decline. We have guests coming, and I wish you to be there."

"But I…"

"Have I asked for anything else?"

"Sure. The, ah…" She glared at him, then stomped her foot. "That is incredibly unfair and low. Don't bring up how nice you've been."

"I negotiate to win."

She grumbled something he couldn't hear, then stalked toward the closet. "Fine. I'll be at your party, but I won't like it. And when I mess up, because it's a *when* not a maybe, you will have to suffer with the consequences. Are you clear on that?"

"Perfectly."

Stupid man, Kiley thought as she stared at the clothes in the closet. Not her real ones—they would never do. Instead she flipped through the fabulous designer clothes Rafiq had purchased for her. Okay, what exactly did one wear to a casual-but-elegant, at-home soirée. She'd never been to a soirée. She'd only ever read about them or seen them on nighttime soap operas.

Panic knotted her stomach and made her a little nauseous. An ambassador. Worse, a woman ambassador. What would they talk about? No doubt Madam Ambassador was ambitious and accomplished. What was Kiley supposed to say in the face of that? "Hi, I'm a twit who put my whole life on hold because I thought I was marrying Mr. Right. When that didn't work out, I became the mistress of a sheik. My entire gender must be so proud."

She sank onto the small padded bench in the closet and hung her head. Okay, maybe that was a little harsh. She'd been stupid about Eric, but not about Rafiq. He was a great guy. She'd gotten the revenge she wanted, a chance to discover the magic between a man and a woman in the most thrilling way possible and time to regroup. He'd been nothing but supportive and kind. The only thing he'd ever asked for, aside from this party, was fidelity.

Plus, there was nothing wrong with wanting to be a wife and mother. Those were still her goals. The difference was she would think things through more next time. She would be more clear about the man she wanted to marry. Character was everything and all that.

She stood and reached for a pair of silk slacks and a fitted white silk blouse. When in doubt, keep it simple, she thought.

After hanging them on the hook by the door, she returned to the bathroom where she quickly applied her makeup. When she'd dressed, she returned to the bedroom. Rafiq was gone, no doubt checking on the last-minute details.

"Couldn't we have started with a couple of clerks and maybe an undersecretary?" she muttered to herself as she walked down the hall. "Maybe a gameskeeper or two?"

She found Rafiq in the dining room. Sana stood next to him, explaining what dishes would go where. When he reached for a bowl of nuts, she slapped his hand. Kiley couldn't help laughing.

"Did you see that?" he asked in outrage. "She violated my royal person."

Sana glared at him. "If you snack now, you won't be hungry later," the housekeeper said, and then returned to the kitchen.

Kiley moved close. "I believe the violations are my responsibility," she whispered in his ear.

He chuckled, then stepped back and studied her outfit. "You look very beautiful. Are you feeling better?"

"A little." She shook her head. "No. Not really. I'm intelligent and fully capable of holding my own in a conversation. I know that. It's just…"

He crossed to her and lightly touched her chin. "You wish to make me proud of you."

She let herself get lost in his dark eyes. "Exactly. If I'd known there was going to be a quiz on current events, I would have studied more."

"There isn't a quiz. This is a few friends getting together."

"Right. That's why we've got the good china out."

He leaned close. "This isn't the good china. That has the state seal on it."

She instantly pictured an aquatic mammal before realizing that probably wasn't the kind of seal he meant. "Casual is good," she said. "I can do casual."

He took her hand and led her to the foyer. They stopped in front of a large mirror.

"You enchant me," he told her, meeting her gaze in the mirror. "You are completely yourself at every turn. You worry about me, you fuss, you create a sense of home where none existed."

"I appreciate the compliment, but I don't think I've done all that."

"You have. Simply by your presence. You have become friends with Sana."

He wasn't making sense. "Who wouldn't? She's great. And she's teaching me to make some really cool dishes."

He smiled. "You take time with people. Now, even though you are nervous, you still show up and intend to do your best. I admire you, Kiley. More than I can say."

He reached into his slacks pocket and pulled out a small box. She recognized the trademark, dark-green leather, the edging in silver, and turned to face him.

"No, no. Not required. I'm not here for the money or the jewelry."

"But I want to give you this."

She rolled her eyes. "Yeah, and last week you gave me a car. Rafiq, stop. I'm not like them. I'm here for a nobler purpose." Because she was falling for him, she thought, knowing she could never say that. Oh, sure, this had started out as a way to get revenge, but it was so much more now.

She felt tears forming and willed them away. He could never know how she had fallen for him. She could stand everything but his pity.

Forcing herself to smile, she said, "I'm here for the sex."

As she expected, he laughed, but he didn't put the box away. "You're going to make me beg, aren't you."

"It's something I've never seen, so probably."

He opened the box. Inside was a diamond pendant. The simple design, three stones, each larger than the one above, took her breath away.

He produced matching earrings from his other pocket. "You know I will win this argument," he told her, even as he handed her the earrings. When she would have refused them, he closed her fingers around them.

"I usually prefer much more obvious pieces," he said. "But I knew those would not suit your delicate beauty. You must admit they're modest by my standards."

The pendant gleamed in the vee of her shirt. She winced as the perfectly cut stones caught the light.

"It's beautiful," she said.

"Then put on the earrings."

She looked at him in the mirror. "I'm not here for jewelry."

"I know. But that reality only makes me want to buy you more."

Rather than argue further, she put on the earrings and admired them. One more item on her list of things she was leaving behind when it was time to go. The car, most of the clothes, any jewelry he bought her—and her heart.

"I was substantially younger than I am now," Margaret Redding, Ambassador to Lucia-Serrat, said with a laugh. "It was my first overseas posting. I'd gotten lucky and been assigned to Rome. There was a fabulous party and there he was, Prince Rafiq."

Kiley smiled at the attractive older woman. "He does clean up well."

"I'll say. We danced, he was charming. It was lust at first sight, for me anyway. At the end of the evening, he was gracious and took my number. I waited weeks for him to call. He never did." She laughed again, then tucked her long auburn hair behind her ears. "I was crushed for at least two days. Then I found out the very handsome prince was at least nine years younger than me. It was hard to tell with him in his tux."

Margaret glanced at Rafiq. "He's grown into quite a man. I envy you." She turned her attention to her husband. "In the purely intellectual sense, of course."

Kiley laughed. "Of course." She'd seen the Reddings come in together and didn't doubt that they were very much in love.

"So how, exactly, did you get to be an ambassador?"

Margaret shifted on the sofa. "I rose through the ranks in the State Department. I was very fortunate in my postings, and I managed to make a good impression on the right people. This is my first time as ambassador and I'm delighted. Lucia-Serrat is a wonderful place to live. I enjoy the people so much and Prince Nasri, Rafiq's father, is very determined to maintain a cordial relationship with the United States." She leaned forward and lowered her voice. "Some days I don't actually feel as if I'm working."

"What does your husband do?"

"He's a writer, which allows him to travel with me. He teases me that it's far more interesting for him to be the dependent spouse than it would be for me. He gets to hang out with all the wives. At my previous post, his team won the embassy golf tournament."

"Do you have children?"

Margaret's smile faded. "No. We talked about it, but with my career, it would have been a challenge. Robert was willing, of course. He would have made an excellent stay-at-home father. But the year we were going to try, I was sent to three different posts in nine months. All that moving around isn't conducive to pregnancy. At least it wasn't for me. And then…"

Margaret stopped and shrugged. "Sorry. I'm rambling. I suppose I'm still thinking about what could have been. I always wanted a career more than a family."

Kiley had trouble believing this attractive, incredibly successful woman could ever doubt her choices. Yet it was clear that Margaret was ambivalent about the road she'd chosen.

"If it makes you feel any better," Kiley said in a lower voice, "I've only ever wanted to be a stay-at-home mom. I've always felt guilty about that, as if I should have big career aspirations."

"I think the fact that I want my career and you want to be a stay-at-home mom and both of us can do that is a wonderful thing. As for feeling guilty—" she touched Kiley's hand "—don't. Isn't it a blessing that you know what you want and have the freedom to pursue it? Isn't that the point?"

"You're right."

Kiley thought about her plans for the future—to find another job, to buy a condo, to live her life fully. If a man came along in the next few years, that would be wonderful. If he didn't, she wasn't going to give up her dream of being a mother. She would find another way.

Margaret glanced over her shoulder to where Rafiq spoke with Robert and another couple.

"He adores you," Margaret told her. "I can see it in his eyes."

"Thank you. I adore him."

Margaret waited expectantly.

Kiley laughed. "You're not going to get me to say any more. We're good friends. We have fun together. That's all." Unfortunately, when the time was up, he would let her go, just as he'd let every other woman go.

"Are you sure?" Margaret asked. "He has to settle down sometime."

"I'm sure he has a princess-in-training all picked out. He's not the boy next door. He has to be very careful about who he chooses."

"Agreed. So why not you?"

Kiley knew all the reasons. She didn't have family connections or the right lineage. Loving him wasn't enough of a calling card.

"She's wonderful," Margaret told Rafiq after dinner. "Where did you find her?"

"She works for me."

Margaret smiled. "Your secretary. Then she's not your usual type."

"Meaning?"

The ambassador laughed. "She's a real person with a heart and a brain. You don't always look for that."

"I would have thought that to be in your position, some measure of diplomacy was required."

Margaret shrugged. "I thought we'd known each other long enough for that not to be an issue. But if you'd prefer I can speak more delicately."

"No. I like that you tell me the truth." He offered

Margaret a glass of cognac, then took one for himself. They were the last ones at the dining room table. Everyone else had gone out to admire the sunset.

She took a sip, then set down her glass. "Your father has been speaking with me. You know he's concerned."

Rafiq could imagine the subject of their conversation. "I'm past thirty and not engaged. It's time for me to take a wife."

"A list has been prepared."

"I trust you didn't bring it with you."

"I wasn't privy to it. I only know of its existence, and that I wasn't on it."

Despite his displeasure at the topic, he smiled. "You tell that story of falling for me all those years ago, but in truth you were far more interested in your career than in any one man."

"Perhaps," she admitted. "But it *is* a good story. Now, back to the subject you don't wish to discuss. I am your friend and I tell you this as a friend. You will be recalled by the end of the year. Your father is determined to see you married with an heir."

He shrugged. "Then I will pick a wife."

"You could sound more enthused about it."

"Why? It is a duty, nothing more."

"What about Kiley?"

The idea had crossed his mind. She was all he had ever wanted. But to marry her was to invite disaster. He would start to believe and have expectations. When she let him down, when she proved she was like all the others and that she could not love with any depth, he would be unable to forgive her. There had been too many disappointments in his life for him to be forgiving now.

"No."

"Want to tell me why not?" she asked.

"Not really. I will pick a suitable bride and produce an heir."

"You don't sound very happy about the prospect. I know you're a prince, Rafiq, but you're also a man. Don't you want to fall madly in love?"

He recalled all that had happened to him while he'd been growing up. All the times he'd been left alone because there was no one to bother. He thought of all the women who claimed to love him when what they loved was the promise of title and untold riches.

"I don't believe in love," he said. "I prefer duty. A desire to serve can be trusted."

"I'm sorry," she said, and touched his hand. "I wish I could change your mind."

"I assure you, I won't."

Kiley walked into the restaurant shortly after twelve. The reservation was for twelve-fifteen, but she didn't want to be late. Actually, she didn't want to be here at all, but if her presence was required, then she would prefer not to be tardy.

Why had she agreed to this? What had she been thinking? In truth, the invitation had been such a shock that she hadn't been able to think of a reason to refuse.

She gave her name to the hostess and was shown to a corner table at the rear of the restaurant. Several of the surrounding tables were still unoccupied. Crystal gleamed on white tablecloths as jacketed servers moved quietly among the upscale clientele.

Kiley adjusted the front of her designer dress. It

wasn't anything she would normally have worn to work, but this wasn't a normal day.

At exactly twelve-sixteen, a beautiful, well-dressed woman approached the table. Kiley stood and offered a tentative smile. The woman looked her up and down.

"So, you're the new flavor of the month. You're not exactly his usual type, are you? Well, sit down." The woman took her seat and motioned to the waiter. "A martini. Very dry. Tell David it's me. He knows what I like."

Carnie Rigby, former beauty queen, former actress and Rafiq's mother, glanced at her. "Let me guess. You'll have white wine."

Kiley figured this had to be some kind of test. No one could be that rude on general principle. At least she hoped not. She leaned back in her seat and turned to the waiter.

"I'll have a glass of iced tea, please."

"Yes, ma'am." The man hurried away.

"Afraid you'll be muddled this afternoon?" Carnie asked as she shrugged off her jacket. "I doubt my son will care."

"He might not, but I would."

"That's the secretary in you. A secretary. Whatever were you thinking? I heard you'd been to college. Surely you could have done more with your life."

Kiley was torn. She'd been raised to respect her elders, and she didn't want to insult Rafiq's mother. But she wasn't willing to be a doormat, either.

"I haven't had a chance to look at the menu," she said, picking up one of the leather-bound pages the waiter had left. "What would you recommend?"

"I really don't care what you eat. You're not going to answer me?"

"Was there a question?"

"I suppose not." Carnie glanced toward the bar. "Where *is* that man with my martini?" She sighed heavily, then turned back to Kiley. "You're living with him."

Kiley hadn't known what to make of the invitation to join Rafiq's mother for lunch. She'd thought maybe the other woman had wanted to get involved in her son's life in some way. Obviously not. Either Carnie saw Kiley as a threat, which was flattering but not true, or she resented anyone her son was involved with. Kiley didn't want to add to her distress, but she refused to be walked on.

"Yes," Kiley said calmly. "It's been a couple of weeks now."

"He doesn't usually invite his women to stay at his house. Did yours burn down?"

Kiley laughed. "No. I believe it's still a perfectly sound structure."

"You do realize this isn't going anywhere, don't you? There's been talk. I may not visit Lucia-Serrat on a regular basis, but I still keep up with the news. His father is displeased that he hasn't taken a wife. It's time for him to marry, and you're getting in the way of that."

Kiley didn't know how much of what she said was true. Rafiq was expected to marry and she wasn't going to be considered a likely candidate. The topic made her uncomfortable, but she refused to let this woman know that.

"I am in Rafiq's life because he has asked me to be," she said carefully. Okay, it was a partial truth. She'd asked to be his mistress and he'd said yes. It was almost the same thing. "As for me being in the way, I'm sorry, but that's not possible. He is a man who does as he pleases. If he wanted me gone so that he could go find a wife, he would simply ask me to leave."

"Perhaps he has and you weren't paying attention."

Kiley thought of the previous night, when he had made love with her for hours. She thought of how they had slept, so closely entwined, their hearts had beat in unison.

"Was there anything else?" she asked. "Another topic, perhaps. Because if your sole purpose for asking me to lunch was to try and bully me into leaving your son, then I must leave."

Carnie's eyes narrowed. "You can't just walk out on me," she snapped. "Who do you think you are?"

"Kiley Hendrick," she said as she rose. "I wish I could say it had been nice to meet you."

Chapter Twelve

Kiley returned to the house and phoned Rafiq to tell him she wasn't coming back to the office that afternoon.

"I'm fine," she said when he asked why. "I'm just feeling a little tired. I'll go in early to clear up whatever I missed today."

"Not necessary," he said. "Are you sure I don't need to call a doctor?"

"Positive. I'm fine. I just need a little time."

"I'll be home later. Perhaps you should rest."

Good idea, she thought as she hung up the phone. But after changing out of her designer clothes and into shorts and a T-shirt, she gave in to the call of the ocean and went out onto the beach.

It was midafternoon, midweek. While there were mothers with children, some teenagers and a few surfers scattered on the sand, for the most part, she had the beach to herself. She walked halfway to the water and settled down, digging her toes deep enough to feel the coolness a few inches down.

The sun was high, the afternoon warm, the waves rhythmic. If she closed her eyes she could smell salt and suntan lotion. The cry of seagulls competed with laughter and an oldies rock station on someone's portable radio.

Her brief encounter with Carnie had carried with it one spark of good news. If she, Kiley, wasn't marrying Rafiq, then she didn't have to worry about Carnie as a mother-in-law. Talk about a miserable person. Kiley still wasn't sure of the point of the meeting. To get rid of her? But how could she be a threat to anyone? Maybe Carnie checked out all Rafiq's women. She would have to ask.

As she stretched out her legs and stared at the ocean, she wondered what her life would have been like if she hadn't found out the truth about Eric. How long would it have taken for her to discover he was pretty much a weasel? And then what? She would have left him. No, this way was better. A quick, clean break that turned out to be much less painful than she would have guessed.

And what about when she left Rafiq? How easy would that be?

She found herself not wanting to think about it, which meant she had to force herself to consider the reality. Their affair *would* end. She could either handle that time gracefully, or she could beg and plead.

Graceful sounded mature, but *pleading* had its place. She supposed the real question was whether or not she would tell him she loved him. It wasn't as much about him wanting to know as her not wanting regrets. Years from now would she want to have told him?

"Still time to decide," she thought.

She closed her eyes and listened to the ocean. The tension eased out of her body as she relaxed. Eventually she leaned back in the sand and let the minutes drift by.

Sometime later she felt a slight prickling down her spine. She sat up and turned to see Rafiq walking toward her. He'd changed into jeans and a shirt and, like her, he hadn't bothered with shoes. He carried a towel or something against his chest.

She rose to her knees and waved at him. As she watched him approach, she felt the love filling her heart and knew she would have to say something before she left. Whether or not it mattered it him, the information was important to her.

"How are you feeling?" he asked as he stopped beside her but didn't sit down.

"Better. I've cleared my head."

"Good." He lowered himself beside her. "I have brought you something."

She rolled her eyes. "Not again. Rafiq, no. You have to stop buying me things. I've told you and told you I'm—"

He cut her off with a kiss. "I think you should stop talking now because when you see what I have, you will not be able to resist."

He drew back the towel and leaned toward her. Kiley stared down at a sleeping pile of white, fluffy fur.

"A puppy," she breathed quietly, wanting to pet it but afraid to wake it up.

"Yes. She is a Maltese. Ten weeks old."

She looked at him. "You bought me a puppy? Why?"

"Because you said you wanted one."

Just like that. Would he get her the moon, too? Tears burned in her eyes, but she blinked them back. No crying, not over something this wonderful.

"I did some research. I thought you would want a small dog, but one with a big personality. She seems quiet now, but trust me, when she is awake, she takes over the room."

Kiley laughed and threw her arm around him. The puppy woke up and immediately began to lick her face.

"Look at you!" Kiley said, scooping her up and holding her out at arm's length. "You're so cute!"

She was all white, except for her black eyes and black nose. Her entire fanny swayed from her enthusiastic tail wagging.

"What a pretty girl," Kiley said as she set the puppy in her lap. The dog immediately tumbled into the sand, stood, shook herself and scrambled back into Kiley's lap.

"She seems to have taken to you," Rafiq said.

"Good, because I adore her." She leaned in and kissed him. "Thank you."

He feigned surprise. "What? No protests, no threats to leave her behind when you go?"

"Nope. She's family."

"Good." He put his arm around her and fingered her hair. "Are you feeling better?"

"Yes." She patted the puppy who promptly flopped onto her back, exposing her tender, pink belly for rubbing. "I wasn't sick, just tired, I guess."

"My mother has that affect on people."

She looked at him. "You told me not to meet her. You warned me she would be difficult."

"And was she?"

"Sort of." She sighed. "Okay, yes. She was difficult and rude and I don't know why she wanted to meet with me. What was the point?"

"What did you discuss?"

"Me? Not much of anything. She knew we were living together, although I don't know how. I didn't think you spoke to her very much."

"I do not."

"That's what I thought. She wanted to make it really clear that our relationship wasn't going anywhere, and she said you were supposed to be getting married and I was in the way of that."

She held her breath after she finished, not sure what he would say back. For a long time there was silence. At last he kissed her neck.

"She's a foolish old woman. I hope you didn't let her upset you too much."

Hmm, that was a neutral. "I tried not to. I told her that if you wanted or needed me out of your life, you would simply tell me."

"True enough. But I don't want you to go. I want you right here."

Just where she wanted to be. "You sure know how to turn a girl's head."

He smiled at her. "Do you doubt my affection?" he asked.

"No. I think you like me a lot."

"Is that enough for you?"

Dangerous, dangerous territory. She could see the flashing red lights all around her. The puppy wiggled to get more comfortable, then closed her eyes. And sighed.

"Yes," Kiley said, knowing it was the closest she'd come to lying to Rafiq. Then, to change the subject, she stood and cradled the puppy in her arms.

"Have you thought this through?" she asked. "Puppies can be a challenge. There's the whole house-training bit, and chewing and all kinds of trouble. Oh, and she'll shed. You live in a really nice place."

"I'll survive," he said. "We may have to bribe Sana, if there is extra cleaning for her."

"Oh, don't worry about that. I'll clean up after this little one."

He reached over and stroked the dog's head. "You'll probably want to take her into work with you while she's so small. A workday is a long time for her to be left alone."

"I'd like that. Thank you."

They walked back to the house, his arm around her. Kiley did her best to remember everything about this moment so that she could have it with her always.

Rafiq knocked on the door of his mother's Century City high-rise.

"This is a surprise," she said as she opened the door for him and returned to the living room. "You don't usually just stop by. I assume there is a purpose."

"There is."

He walked into the large, airy condo. The windows faced north, giving him a view of west Los Angeles, Brentwood and Hollywood in the distance.

She sat down and picked up a tumbler filled with clear liquid and ice. "Would you like something to drink?"

"No, thank you."

He crossed the pale carpeting and sat across from the woman who had given birth to him. From the time he could remember until he graduated from university in England, he'd seen her fewer than a half-dozen times. Once he'd grown and, as she had put it on his twenty-third birthday when she'd thrown a party for him, gotten interesting, she wanted to be a part of his life.

By then it had been too late for him. He was willing to treat her with some measure of respect—she *was* his mother—but that was all.

He suspected she used her connection to him when it was convenient, although that came with a price. To claim to be the mother of a prince meant admitting her age—something he knew she hated to do.

She was attractive, he acknowledged. Doctors had worked their magic to keep her skin tight and unlined. She dressed well, could converse on many subjects and knew the value of any antique, piece of jewelry or fine art. In many ways, she reminded him of a snake: cold-blooded, keeping to the shadows and intent only on survival.

"It's about the girl, isn't it?" Carnie said with a sigh. "I knew right away she was going to be tiresome."

"Leave her alone," Rafiq said. "You are to have no further contact with her. I don't know what game you're playing but I won't be a part of it."

His mother sipped her drink. She wore a pale shirt tucked into tailored slacks. Her small feet were bare, her toes painted. She was the epitome of at-home elegance.

"My, my. I don't recall you being so protective about one of your women before," she said with a smile. "How touching." She set down her drink. "But honestly, Rafiq, is she all that different? At night, when you reach for her, couldn't she be one of a hundred different bodies?"

"I meant what I said. Leave her alone."

"Are you threatening me?"

"Yes."

His mother seemed unfazed by the statement, but he suspected it was posturing on her part. They both knew there was damage to be done. Should it come out that she had been snubbed by her own son, invitations would not flow so freely. The rich and famous would be less inclined to frequent her exclusive gallery.

"Interesting." His mother gazed at him. "And this one matters why?"

"I'm not going to discuss that with you."

"Of course not. You wouldn't want to risk me offering advice. What if it made sense? You couldn't possibly take it, because it came from me, and then where would you be?"

"I'm not a child who feels the need to rebel against you," he told her.

"That's true. You're a man. A prince. Your father's heir. Are you aware that Kiley is in love with you?"

The question slammed into him with the subtlety of a California earthquake. He felt the floor shift, shake, then settle back into place.

In love with him? Kiley? It wasn't possible. She could not be.

"Unlikely," he said, keeping his turmoil safely inside.

His mother laughed. "Oh, my dear. You may be all grown-up but you're still a man and blind where women are concerned. Of course she's in love with you. What did you expect? She's your secretary." She paused and nodded slowly. "Yes, I know that. I know more than you think. I know that before you, she was engaged and he was quite the jerk. So she came to you, all sad and broken and you offered to fix her. How kind."

That wasn't what had happened, but he wasn't about to correct her.

"Did you honestly think she was like your other women?" Carnie asked mockingly. "Did you think she would understand the rules and play by them? If so, you were mistaken. She's the kind of woman who leads with her heart, the poor fool. I'm sure she's saying all the right things, but trust me, she is desperately in love with you."

He didn't want to know that. Part of him started to dismiss his mother's words out of hand. Kiley had known him for a long time. She'd seen the other women in his life, was clear on how the process worked. She wouldn't break the rules.

And yet… He couldn't ignore what Carnie said simply because he didn't like the messenger.

"What happens when you walk away?" his mother asked. "For you, she is simply one more conquest, but for her you are her prince. I mean that in the literal sense as well as the figurative. I can't blame her and you shouldn't, either. Look at her life, Rafiq. Look at what you have shown her, done with her. How could she resist? It's not her fault. But it's very sad. Imagine how her life will be when you tire of her. Who will pick up the pieces of her shattered heart then?"

He didn't believe in love, not for himself. He couldn't imagine ever trusting that much. But he knew it existed. He'd seen tiny lights in the darkness, places where people truly gave all they had for another. He'd seen signs of love at Kiley's family's house. In the laughter, the hugs, the memories.

"What is your point?" he asked his mother.

"I just wanted to warn you that you were treading on dangerous territory with Kiley. She's such a sweet girl."

He narrowed his gaze. "And?"

"And I've heard rumors. Your father isn't all that happy with you these days. You're over thirty, Rafiq. It's time you married."

"I see. Let me guess. You have a candidate in mind."

"Yes, as a matter of fact, I do. The daughter of a friend. She's a wonderful young woman. Very beautiful and accomplished. She's extremely well educated and has an advanced degree in music. She plays the violin. I would like to set up a meeting between the two of you. Nothing too stressful. Perhaps a brunch this weekend or next."

He stood. "I'm not interested in the relative of anyone who would call you a friend. If nothing else, I would be forced to question her judgment."

Carnie glared at him. "You're going to have to marry someone, and we both know it's not going to be that fool you're sleeping with. She's a nobody. Who are her parents? What lineage or talent would she bring to that match? Who would your children be?"

She continued to talk, but he wasn't listening. He turned and walked out of her condo, then turned toward the elevator. One word repeated over and over in his head.

Children.

He and Kiley had been lovers for three weeks. In that time he'd taken her several times a day, making love with her until they were both exhausted. Yes, he had used protection…every time but one…the first time.

She'd been a virgin, inexperienced and unprepared. He'd been around her enough to know she wasn't on The Pill.

One time, he told himself. Only one time. Yet she could be pregnant. Condoms weren't foolproof.

He stepped onto the elevator and pushed the button for the parking garage. He was Prince Rafiq of Lucia-Serrat. If there was a child, there was only one thing for him to do.

Kiley sat curled up on the sofa, reading. When she heard the garage door open, followed by the low purr of Rafiq's car, she did her best to continue to concentrate on her book, but she wasn't fooling anyone. Her stomach clenched, her toes curled and everything in her body went on the alert.

She wanted to stand up and shout, "He's home! He's home!" But that seemed silly, what with the entire population of the house currently consisting of herself and the puppy, and the latter had already scampered for the door off the kitchen where she would dance and whine until her pack leader came in and acknowledged her.

Kiley knew she had it bad when she felt a slight flash of jealousy, knowing the puppy would get the first bit of attention. Then she decided to be mature, because that night she would have Rafiq in her bed.

"I'm home," he called as he walked into the house.

"Hi," she said back, and wondered if he made any announcement when he walked into the official residence back on Lucia-Serrat. Or was there some town-crier type who ran ahead telling all that Prince Rafiq had returned?

He came in carrying the puppy. "She gets far too excited about my arrival," he said. "If she spins much harder or faster, she'll injure herself."

"She's happy to see you," Kiley said, willing to do a little spinning herself.

She walked up to him and kissed him. The puppy yipped happily at being caught in the middle and tried to lick them both.

She laughed and took her from Rafiq. "You're a little crazy person, aren't you?" She glanced at him. "I've named her."

He took her free hand and led her to the sofa. "What did you decide?"

"Fariha. It's Arabic. It means—"

"Joyful or happy. I speak Arabic."

She grinned. "Of course you do. I thought the name was appropriate and we can call her Fari for short."

She sank onto the sofa and held Fari up in the air. "Do you like your new name?" she asked the puppy. "Don't you think it's as pretty as you?"

Fari wiggled and yipped her approval. Kiley set her on the floor and watched her scamper to her chew toy by the window.

"How was your meeting?" she asked.

"Interesting." He stared at her. "Are you happy here, Kiley?"

"What?" Silly man. "Of course I am."

He took one of her hands in his and kissed her palm. "I know things have moved quickly between us. Becoming lovers, you moving in."

Was he worried about her? "I'm fine with all that. I like being here. You're a pretty fun date."

"How flattering. Do you love me?"

The question came from nowhere and knocked the air right out of her. She didn't know what to think, what do say. Heat flared on her cheeks as she realized that he must have guessed. Somehow she'd given herself away.

"I, ah…" She pressed her lips together. "Rafiq, I don't understand."

"It's a simple question. Do you love me?"

Panic joined embarrassment. He hated that she'd fallen for him. She'd broken all the rules and he wanted her out of here. Oh, but she wasn't ready to go. Not yet. They still had more time together.

She wanted to protest, to promise to do better. She wanted a lot of things, but wanting something didn't always make it come true. So she drew in a deep breath and looked directly into his dark eyes.

"Yes, Rafiq. I'm in love with you. But before you panic, I want you to know this doesn't change anything. I understood the rules when I first asked to be your mistress and I still understand them."

She couldn't tell what he was thinking. She thought he might be on the verge of smiling, but wasn't sure. He didn't seem angry or upset, so that was good.

"Some rules are made to be broken," he told her, and stunned her by pulling a ring out of his shirt pocket.

Not just any ring, either. This was a huge, sparkling diamond solitaire that looked very much like an engagement ring. The hits kept on coming, then he slid off the sofa onto one knee and smiled at her.

"Kiley, will you marry me?"

She blinked. "Excuse me?"

He laughed. "What is so confusing about the question? I have asked you to be my wife."

Okay, it sounded like English. She was fairly sure she understood all the words, but the sentence itself didn't make any sense.

Yet there he was, on his knees, holding out an engagement ring. What was that old saying? If it looks like a duck and walks like a duck then it's probably a duck.

"You're proposing," she said, just to be completely sure.

"Apparently not very well."

"To me."

"Yes. The only other female in this room is the dog and I assure you I have no interest in her except as a pet."

"You want to marry me."

"Yes."

There was a sliver of doubt, a voice that whispered stuff like this didn't happen to regular people and yet here it was. In the flesh, so to speak.

Happiness bubbled up inside of her until she felt light enough to float away.

"You're not kidding?" she asked, just to be sure.

He leaned forward and kissed her. "On my honor, I very much wish you to marry me."

"Okay, then," she said before she shrieked her excitement, wrapped both arms around him and said, "Yes."

Chapter Thirteen

Rafiq had wondered if he would have second thoughts, but none appeared. Their conversation the next day only reinforced his decision.

"Do you have to tell your parents?" she asked from the large leather chair in his study at the house. "I don't think they'll approve."

She looked so charmingly worried that he found it difficult not to cross to her and kiss away the small frown between her eyebrows.

"You are well educated, articulate, kind and very much in love with their son. Why would they not approve?"

She sighed. "This isn't a time for logic. Besides, that argument isn't going to work with your mother, who, for reasons I can't explain, already hates me."

"She has her own agenda for my future," he said, remembering his conversation with Carnie. "It has nothing to do with who you are."

"A sentiment that isn't as comforting as one might think. As for your father, I'm your basic commoner. Won't he have been hoping for minor European royalty at the very least?"

He smiled. "What do you know of my stepmother?"

"She's very pretty and has two daughters."

"And before she married my father, she was a poor orphan who dreamed of becoming a nurse."

"Really?" Kiley straightened in her chair. "That makes me feel better. You swear she's nice?"

"You will like her very much."

"I just wish you didn't have to tell them."

"They would notice eventually. Besides, what of your parents? They may not approve."

Kiley laughed. "Oh, yeah. Every parent gets totally bummed out to hear his or her daughter is marrying a prince. What a drag."

"They may not appreciate me taking you away. Within a couple of years we will have to move to Lucia-Serrat."

She nodded. "I know, and I'm okay with that." She leaned down and petted Fari who had curled up on the chair's ottoman. "You hear that, sweet face? We're going to Lucia-Serrat where you get to run around in a palace and be a royal dog. Like a puppy princess." Kiley glanced at Rafiq. "Speaking of the whole princess thing, any way I can pass on that?"

"What do you mean?"

"Just that I'm really happy to marry you and all, but the whole being-in-the-public-eye, I'm-the-princess thing really doesn't work for me. I could stay in the background. No one would have to know."

If he hadn't been sure before, her question would have reassured him. He couldn't imagine Carmen or any of the other women he'd been involved with ever wishing *not* to be named a princess. For them, that was the point.

"It is part of the deal," he said. "Does that change your mind?"

She wrinkled her nose. "It's not my favorite part, but I'll survive."

He believed her and in that moment, he found hope. She was the right woman for him, a woman who led with her heart and gave unconditionally. She would be a good mother to their children.

He wanted to be sure she would love them as she had been loved. He knew she would never leave them. There was no temptation he could offer that would cause her to leave them behind. As it was, she barely let Fari out of her sight. How much more would she care when she had a baby?

He glanced at her still-flat stomach. Was she pregnant? Did his child grow there, even now? Time would tell. He doubted the thought had occurred to her and he preferred it that way. Better for them to get much closer to the wedding before she found out she was pregnant. He didn't want her questioning the timing of his proposal.

"I will call my parents later this evening," he said. "I'm sure they will want to fly out and meet you."

She curled back up in the chair. "There goes my good mood."

"You will like them and they will like you."

"Uh-huh." She didn't sound convinced. "Then

they're going to want to meet my parents, and even if they don't, my folks will want to meet them. We're going to have to have some kind of group parental meeting. Let's do that here rather than in Sacramento."

"A brunch," he said, appreciating the irony of borrowing his mother's idea.

"Oh, that would work. It's less formal."

"We'll have to make an announcement to the press, as well. That will come from my father's office, but we must make sure your family knows before they read about it in a magazine."

"Good point."

"There are other considerations," he said. "The wedding will have to be a formal state event."

She practically writhed in her chair. "Yeah, I guessed that was the case. I saw the British royal family's weddings on television. It won't be that big, will it?"

"No. There will be four or five hundred guests, about half of whom are dignitaries."

Kiley wasn't sure how much more of this she could take. The idea of a formal, state wedding made her stomach hurt. She didn't want to be a princess, a figurehead or anything the least bit official. She wanted to marry Rafiq, stay in this house and have babies.

But that wasn't going to be the plan. He wasn't just some guy she'd fallen for—he was Prince Rafiq of Lucia-Serrat—a fact that had been interesting but not especially important until he'd slid the ring on her finger.

She glanced down at the sparkling diamond. She could never have imagined her dreams coming true this way. The most she'd allowed herself to fantasize about was his extending their affair. But marriage? How did she ever get so lucky?

"I haven't the faintest idea how to plan a royal wedding," she said.

"I know. After I tell my parents, I'll have someone trained in such matters flown out. While the wedding itself will be on the island, we can do the planning from here."

Which sounded lovely, but she had a feeling that Rafiq was going to be a typical male. There wouldn't be so much "we" in the wedding planning as there would be "her."

"There are probably a lot of rules we have to follow?" she asked.

"Some. The ceremony will be in the main church on the island, and the reception is held at the crown prince's royal residence."

"At least I don't have to go hunting for locations."

His expression softened. "Did you have somewhere special in mind?"

"No." She hadn't allowed herself to consider it. Not with him. "I'm okay with tradition as long as someone can tell me what's expected."

"I assure you, the wedding planner will be very clear on that. However, you must be willing to stand up to him. There are traditions, but this is also your wedding. I wish you to make it everything you want it to be. Don't give in on what's important. I can't know your mind unless you speak it, Kiley. Tell me if you're having trouble getting through to him and I will intervene."

"Thanks, but I'll be okay." Dealing with the wedding planner could be her initial princess-in-training test. She intended to pass the first time.

"We have to talk about your job."

Kiley started to protest, then pressed her lips together. "You're saying it's not appropriate for your future wife to be your secretary?"

"Something like that."

"But I like working for you."

"And I enjoy having you in the office. To be honest, you're the most efficient assistant I've had in a long time. I don't want to make a change, but your priorities must be elsewhere."

He made sense. Once word of their engagement got out, she would be busy with other things. She wasn't sure what, but no doubt she would find out in time. If nothing else, she would have to learn about Lucia-Serrat. She knew a little of the island by virtue of working for Rafiq, but not enough to represent it as the princess.

Kiley still had trouble getting her mind around that concept. A princess? Her? And yet it came with marrying Rafiq.

While she was on the subject of improbabilities, what about the engagement? As much as she'd fallen in love with him, she'd never dreamed he would return her affection and want to make things permanent. It was as if every dream she'd ever had had come true.

"What are you thinking about?" he asked. "You have the most intriguing smile."

"Do I?" Her smile widened. "I was thinking how lucky I am. I love you so much and I was heartbroken at the thought of having to leave."

He stood and moved toward her. "And now?"

She rose. "Now I get to stay forever."

He reached for her. She went into his arms with a

practiced ease. They had made love so many times in the past few weeks that there was a sense of the familiar. Yet at the same time, everything felt new and delicious.

Even as he began to kiss her, she felt herself needing him. Her body melted, heated, swelled and readied for his sensual assault.

When he tilted his head and claimed her with his tongue, she parted instantly. She danced with him, claiming him herself with a nip on his lower lip.

He chuckled low in his throat, then bent down and pressed his mouth to her neck. She let her head fall back as her stomach clenched and her breasts tightened in anticipation.

"I want you," he breathed against her skin.

"I'm yours."

She was. For always.

As he sucked on the curve where her neck met her shoulder, she unfastened the buttons of his shirt. He nudged her back until she bumped into the desk. Once there, it was a simple matter to straighten, pull off her T-shirt and let him shove down her shorts and panties. She was already barefoot.

He shrugged out of his shirt while she unfastened her bra. Then she was naked before him. He looked at her body, his gaze lingering on her breasts before dropping to the blond curls below her belly.

She could see his erection pressing against his slacks and the rapid rise and fall of his chest. Knowing he wanted her made her want him more. When he put his hands on her waist, she pushed off the floor and landed on the edge of the desk.

The wood was cool on her bare skin, but also erotic.

But she barely noticed. He bent down and took her right nipple in his mouth as he reached between her legs.

She parted for him, pulling her thighs as far apart as she could, wanting him to touch her everywhere. His fingers rubbed her swollen flesh, then settled into a steady rhythm designed to make her his slave.

He rubbed that single point of pleasure with his thumb and pushed two fingers deep inside of her. At the same time, he sucked on her nipple, then licked the tight point and blew on her damp skin.

So much pleasure, she thought, barely able to form coherent thoughts. She clutched at him, never wanting him to stop, needing him, only him. Tension built, as did the promise of her release. She fumbled with his belt and slacks, desperate to have him inside of her.

He straightened and quickly stripped off the rest of his clothes. Then he moved between her legs and pushed into her.

He filled her deeply, moving slowly, letting her stretch to accommodate him. The slow aching gave way to more frantic desire. She needed movement to climax. The deep, thrilling thrusts as he made her his own.

He obliged her by withdrawing, then slipping in again. More quickly this time. She sank back on the desk and gave herself over to the act of love they shared.

He clutched her hips to pull her against him. Need grew. She wrapped her legs around him, holding them more closely together. Tension increased.

She felt her breathing quicken as her body heated. He slipped his hand between them and rubbed that most sensitive place.

It was too much, she thought as she cried out her

pleasure. Her orgasm washed over her, blanking her mind until there was only sensation. She grabbed for him, pulling him in deeper and deeper, taking all of him, riding him until he, too, lost control and they came together in a shuddering climax.

"I've never been to Los Angeles before," Princess Phoebe said from the back of the limo. She touched her husband's arm. "Maybe we'll have time to go to a theme park while we're here."

Rafiq didn't say anything, but he held in a smile. He doubted his father would ever consider going to a place like that on purpose, but he would deny his wife nothing. They'd been together nearly fifteen years and from all accounts seemed happy.

Something to consider, he told himself. Perhaps he and Kiley could be like that, as well, growing in respect and affection over the years. Why was love required?

Prince Nasri patted his wife's hand. "We'll see," he said. "It can be difficult to arrange visits like that on short notice. The park must be closed and—"

Phoebe leaned close and smiled. "We don't have to close the park. Trust me. No one here will have any idea who we are. A few bodyguards will be enough." She turned to Rafiq. "Tell him it's perfectly safe."

Rafiq held up his hands. "That is for my father to decide."

She sighed. "How typical. You haven't seen each other in nearly six months and still you band together to side against me."

Her words were serious, but Rafiq saw the sparkle of amusement in her eyes.

"I'm not willing to make a claim for your safety until I'm sure," he said.

"Very sensible," his father told him. "Speaking of which, who is this girl you want to marry. What do you know about her?"

"Enough," Rafiq said, knowing their few moments of rapport would end now.

Nasri frowned. "There are many well-qualified young women you have yet to meet."

"Yes. I'm sure you have a list."

"We do. If you're interested."

Phoebe took her husband's hand and squeezed. "Now don't get all huffy and regal with Rafiq. I'm sure he's chosen well."

"Yes, but *who* is she?"

"Who was I?" Phoebe asked.

"Someone I adored from the moment I saw you."

"A nobody," she reminded him. "I had no family, no connection to anyone powerful. I hadn't even gone to college."

"That was different," he said, and lightly kissed her.

"This is different, too," she told him. "If Rafiq loves her, then that is enough."

The conversation reaffirmed Rafiq's decision that Kiley should wait to meet his father at the house. Far better for her to be relaxed and for Nasri to voice his concerns out of her earshot. Besides, it didn't matter what his father said. He and Kiley *would* be married.

The prince looked unconvinced. "She is of good character?"

Rafiq nodded. "Intelligent, caring, loyal and very kind. She will be a good mother to my sons."

"And your daughters," Phoebe said with a sigh. "What is it about you men and your sons? It's very annoying. Rafiq, I assure you, your father loves his daughters as much as his sons. You need not fear that they're ignored."

"I am relieved," he said, keeping his thoughts to himself. With Phoebe there to watch over her children, he had no doubt his father participated in their upbringing.

But it had been different for him. Prince Nasri had disappeared from his son's life and had rarely returned. Rafiq could remember months passing without a word. Birthdays and holidays were frequently spent in the company of nannies and tutors. When he'd been old enough to go to boarding school, most of his vacations had been spent there. It wasn't until he'd turned thirteen that his father had decided it was time for Rafiq to learn about his future duties.

They drove up the driveway. Phoebe smiled.

"I love this house. It reminds me a little of Lucia-Serrat, and yet it's completely different. You have the best of both worlds here."

"Is that why my son and heir chooses to stay away for so long?" Nasri asked with a grumble.

Phoebe shook her head. "Be nice. You promised. Part of the reason your son stays away is you're an old grouch most of the time. You're not yet fifty, but you have the temperament of a man close to eighty." She glanced at Rafiq. "Except when he is with the girls. Then he is happy and carefree. I suppose it's the responsibility."

Arnold, the driver, opened the rear door and she slid out.

"You will be a big help when you return," she told Rafiq as she stood on the driveway and smoothed her long, blond hair. "We are both looking forward to that."

"As am I," Rafiq said, speaking the truth. He missed Lucia-Serrat. Now that he would marry Kiley and start a family, he found himself ready to return.

The front door opened. Kiley stepped out and smiled.

"Hello," she said. "It's lovely to have you here."

Rafiq saw the terror in her eyes and knew that she would rather be anywhere but here. Still, he doubted Nasri or Phoebe noticed.

She'd dressed in a pale-blue dress that fell loosely to her calves. Her makeup was light, her jewelry conservative. She hadn't discussed her clothing with him, and he was pleased by her choice. She looked exactly right for the occasion. He could also imagine her brushing close and whispering to him that she wasn't wearing any underwear.

"You must be Kiley," Phoebe said, stepping forward and holding out both her hands. "I'm delighted to meet you. At last someone has captured Rafiq's heart. I'd begun to lose hope."

Kiley laughed as the two women hugged. "He sure has dated a lot. I like to think he got it out of his system."

"Nasri did the same thing," Phoebe said in a mock whisper. "I believe it makes him appreciate me more." She turned to her husband and drew him near. "Here she is. Don't you adore her right away?"

Rafiq moved next to Kiley and put his hand on the small of her back. "Kiley, this is my father, Prince Nasri Majin of Lucia-Serrat."

Kiley offered a very impressive curtsy. "It is very much an honor to meet you, sir."

Rafiq watched as his father looked her over. He wasn't concerned—family opinion mattered little to him—but he wanted the meeting to go well for Kiley's sake.

At last his father smiled. "Welcome to our family, Kiley."

"Thank you."

Rafiq started to say they should all go inside, but before he could speak the words, Fari burst through the open door and began running in circles around everyone. She yapped and spun and shook with delight.

"Oh, no." Kiley reached for her but couldn't catch her. "She's our new puppy. I locked her up in the bedroom. How did she get out?"

Phoebe laughed. "She's a wonder."

"She's just a puppy," Kiley said. "And still a little excitable."

"Here." Prince Nasri reached for her.

"Oh, you don't want to do that," Kiley said, sounding worried. "When she gets excited, she—"

It was too late. Nasri picked up the puppy and brought her to his chest. Fari licked his chin and promptly peed down the front of his shirt.

Chapter Fourteen

Kiley and Phoebe sat out on the deck the following afternoon. Fari stretched out at Kiley's feet and dozed in the sunlight.

"It's beautiful here," Phoebe said. "The first time I saw pictures of Rafiq's house I remember thinking that he'd wanted to keep a piece of Lucia-Serrat with him. While the view is different, the essence of the place is very similar."

"He misses the island," Kiley told her. Not that he talked about it that much, but she had a strong sense of his need to return home.

"And we miss him." Phoebe smiled at her. "I adore my stepchildren. They're all so wonderful. And they seem to like me, which is great. I would have hated to be wicked and live up to that horrible stepmother cliché."

Kiley laughed. "I'm not sure you could be wicked if you tried."

"Probably not, but I do a great crabby. Just ask my husband."

Kiley knew that the princess was in her early thirties, but she looked much younger. Perhaps it was the air of contentment that seemed to surround her, as if she had everything she'd ever wanted.

"Do you miss your girls?" she asked.

Phoebe nodded. "That's the only bad part of traveling. We were going to bring them, but there was a very special sleep-over planned, and that seemed much more interesting to them. Plus, I wanted to have time to get to know you, which wouldn't have happened with my girls around. They're very energetic."

Kiley felt a whisper of envy. She wanted children and soon. Would Rafiq be happy if she got pregnant right away?

"The island is a wonderful place to grow up," Phoebe said. "There's so much for children to do, yet everything is so safe. I couldn't have picked better if I'd tried."

"It sounds lovely. I'm looking forward to seeing it firsthand. Although maybe as a tourist rather than a future princess."

Phoebe's expression turned sympathetic. "A little nervous?"

"More than a little. There's so much to learn. I had to quit my job because it would have been too weird to be engaged and working for Rafiq. I was terrified I wouldn't have anything to do. Instead I'm busy all the time. I'm studying the history of the island so I understand the people. Then there's all the protocol, customs, expectations. It's a lot to take in. I want to be a good wife. I want Rafiq to be proud of me."

"I can see that and I admire your energy. But isn't loving him going to be enough?"

"You'd think," Kiley said, wishing it were. "It's my problem, not his. Rafiq has never asked me to learn anything or change." But she was afraid he would be disappointed if she wasn't the perfect princess.

"You're lucky," Phoebe said. "You won't be the wife of the crown prince for many years. That will give you a certain amount of freedom."

"I know. It must have been difficult for you to step right into that role."

Phoebe shrugged. "I was young and so very much in love. I would have done anything for Nasri. By the time I knew enough to be scared, I knew enough to get by. Then I got pregnant, and once I became a mother, the rest of it didn't seem so important." She touched Kiley's arm. "Don't worry. You'll do well, and Rafiq will be there to guide you."

"Thank you." Kiley did trust that Rafiq would be a help. "You're being very kind."

"I have an ulterior motive."

Kiley couldn't imagine what she could have that the other woman wanted. "Which is?"

"I want to know if Rafiq has said anything about his father." She held up a hand. "I know I'm prying and it's terrible of me, but I do so worry about those two. They've never been close and I know that hurts them both. I kept thinking that as Rafiq got older their differences would fade away, but they haven't. There is a distance between them. I'm sure you've noticed it."

Kiley nodded slowly. She didn't want to be having this conversation. As much as she liked Phoebe, she wasn't going to betray Rafiq by sharing what he'd told her about his father.

"I know Rafiq enjoys his work," Kiley said carefully. "And he looks forward to returning home."

Phoebe smiled. "It's all right. In your position I wouldn't have said anything, either. I just wish…" She stared out at the ocean. "I wish things had been different. Nasri was so young when Rafiq was born. Still only seventeen. He wanted to go off to university in England, to grow up and have a life. He had the means to hire staff to look after Rafiq and so he did. He never saw the importance of being a father. He didn't think about a young child left alone."

Kiley didn't want to think about it, either. It broke her heart to imagine Rafiq as a small boy, abandoned by both his parents.

"As Nasri grew, he fell in love and married. I'm sure his first wife tried with Rafiq, but soon she had children of her own. After she died, Nasri lost himself in grief. By the time he surfaced, Rafiq was away at boarding school. There was never a good time."

"Perhaps the prince should have made time," Kiley said before she could stop herself. "He was the father."

"I agree," Phoebe told her. "As does Nasri. He sees the mistakes he made, but they are in the past and impossible to rectify. I wish I could make you see how much he wants to be close to his son."

Kiley didn't like being put in this position, but before she could protest, Phoebe shook her head.

"Enough of such seriousness. At least the cycle will

be broken. Rafiq will be a better father to his children and you will be there for them as well. I can already feel the love between you."

Kiley smiled. "Does it show?"

"You light up when he walks in the room, but isn't that as it should be?"

She thought about how happy he made her and knew she wouldn't change anything. "Yes, it is."

Kiley did her best not to look at herself in the mirror. Seeing herself in formal clothing would only make her more nervous.

"How did they do it so quickly?" she asked, not really expecting an answer. "It's a formal event. Shouldn't that take weeks?"

"Phoebe is very good at putting parties together."

"Lucky us."

Kiley concentrated on her breathing and did her best not to throw up. Telling herself she shouldn't worry, that this was exactly like the big fund-raiser she'd attended with Rafiq only a month ago, was a big fat lie. It wasn't the same at all. Then she'd been one of a hundred guests. Today she was one of two guests of honor, as the party was to celebrate her official engagement to Rafiq.

There was too much to think about. What she was supposed to say when she greeted people. How could she remember the words to the national anthem of Lucia-Serrat? Or to make sure to keep smiling because everyone would be watching? She also had to worry about what she was going to wear for her official portrait, and the wedding planner, who was arriving in a matter of days, and the fact that they were leaving Fari alone for the whole evening and who knew what trouble she would get into.

"I should stay here with the puppy," she said.

Rafiq stepped out of the bathroom. He wore a tailored tuxedo and looked so handsome, he took her breath away. He crossed to her, took her hands in his and kissed her fingers.

"I'm afraid I can't allow that. People would not understand why my fiancée wasn't at my side. It would cause a scandal."

"I guess."

"You will do well," he told her.

"Do you promise?"

"Yes."

If only she could be as sure. "You're used to this sort of thing. For me it's all very nerve-racking. I think I need to lie down."

He chuckled and pulled her close. "You make me very happy."

"You say that now, but after I say something inappropriate you're going to be giving me a stern talking-to."

"Relax, Kiley. There is nothing to worry about."

She drew in a breath, then released it. Staring up into his dark eyes she said, "You know I'm only doing this for you, right? You believe that I have no interest in the actual princess thing."

"You've made that very clear."

"And you know that I love you."

His smile never wavered. "I know you give with your whole heart and that you mean what you say with all that you are."

Some of her tension eased away. "Okay. Good.

Sometimes I worry that you can't really bring yourself to trust me or anyone." She shrugged. "I talked to Phoebe a little about your father. I think he wants to improve the relationship he has with you."

Rafiq released her instantly. "Did she say that? Did you listen and agree to discuss this with me?"

"No. It wasn't like that. I didn't take her side. Actually, I didn't say much of anything. But I couldn't stop thinking about what she said, and it makes me sad that the two of you aren't close. He's your father, your family. We'll be moving back to Lucia-Serrat in a few years and you're going to be working with him. Wouldn't that be easier if you got along?"

Rafiq turned his back to her. "You don't know what you're talking about."

"I don't know the details, but I understand the circumstances. He was wrong. Very wrong, but he was also young. Just seventeen. How smart were you at that age?"

"Do not involve yourself in things that are not your concern," he said, his voice a low growl.

"This is my concern because I love you. I hate to see you hurt by this."

He spun to face her. "I am not hurt. None of this touches me. You are wrong if you think I mourn a relationship we never had."

"I don't believe you."

"Then you are a fool. We will not speak of this any longer."

He stated the command as if he fully expected her obedience. He had never been angry with her, and while she didn't like it, she wasn't going to let him dictate to her.

"You don't get to decide that," she said softly.

His gaze narrowed. "What did you say?"

"You don't get to say what we will or will not talk about. That's a joint decision and I think this is an important conversation."

"Then it is one you will have with yourself because we will not speak of it again."

He turned to leave, but before he got more than halfway across the room, Sana appeared.

"The car is here," she said, "and your parents are waiting."

Rafiq nodded his thanks, then turned to Kiley. "Are you ready?"

Just like that? They weren't going to finish their conversation?

She collected her purse and followed him through the house. A part of her wanted to insist they continue talking, but she knew this wasn't the time. Not with his parents waiting and an official state party to attend. But it made her uncomfortable to have unfinished business with him.

The drive to the hotel was uncomfortable for her, mostly because she was aware of how much Rafiq *wasn't* speaking. But Phoebe and Prince Nasri chatted and Kiley did her best to relax.

When they arrived, she was unprepared for the number of photographers lined up outside of the hotel. There had to be close to a hundred. Panic seized her, making it impossible to breathe.

"We'll wait for the bodyguards," Prince Nasri said.

Phoebe shook her head. "I don't understand the fascination. On a day-to-day basis, my life is very normal."

Kiley gave a strangled laugh. Normal? Phoebe was

a princess. They were royalty. And she was so not ready to be a part of that.

Rafiq glanced at her. "Are you all right?"

"No," she croaked, barely able to form the word.

"Nerves?"

She nodded.

"I can cure them."

He bent down and pressed his mouth to hers. The kiss was hot, long and very demanding. She felt her anxiety fade away as passion took its place. His tongue claimed her and taunted her until she could only think of her need.

He shifted and pressed his mouth to her ear.

"I want you."

Desire made her shiver. The rear door of the limo opened and the night exploded as dozens of flashes went off, but all she could think about was Rafiq.

The walk into the hotel ballroom passed in a blur. When their party stepped inside, the orchestra immediately began playing the Lucia-Serrat national anthem, followed by the one for the United States. At the end, Prince Nasri stepped up to the microphone and welcomed everyone to the event.

Later, when they were at last free to escape to the dance floor, Kiley smiled at Rafiq. "You rescued me."

"The situation can be intimidating. You'll get used to it."

"I doubt that, but thank you, anyway." She bit her lower lip. "Does this mean we're no longer fighting?"

"We never were."

That surprised her. "What would you call it, then?"

"A conversation of little consequence."

She didn't like the sound of that. They'd had a serious disagreement. Their first. Sure, it was bound to happen and she was okay with that. She just wasn't sure she liked him denying it had ever taken place. Had he not been affected or did he simply not care enough to worry? And did she really want to know which it was?

The evening passed in a blur of dancing, introductions and speeches. Kiley found herself feeling both welcomed by the guests and uncomfortable with being the center of attention. Phoebe assured her she would get used to it, but Kiley couldn't imagine that happening. Still, two months ago she would never have imagined marrying a prince, either, so who was she to say?

She excused herself from a large group and made her way toward the restroom. As she entered a quiet hallway, she felt someone touch her arm. She turned and was stunned to see Eric standing there.

"Why are you here?" she asked, sure this couldn't be good, and uncomfortable to be seen speaking with him.

"I had to talk to you."

Oh, please. Was he really going to make a fuss now? "Eric, go away. There's nothing between us."

"I don't care about that," he told her. "I'm here because I'm worried about you."

"That's a new one."

"You're making a terrible mistake. Everything is happening too fast. You don't love this guy and he doesn't love you. You're reacting to what happened between us."

He took her hand and stared into her eyes. "I can't tell you how sorry I am about that. I was such a jerk."

She pulled free of his touch. "*Jerk* doesn't begin to describe it. I don't know why you're here, Eric, but it's time for you to leave. You're a cheat and a liar and I'm glad to be rid of you."

She walked back toward the ballroom. She had a feeling that if she went into the ladies' room now, Eric would simply follow her, and she didn't need that kind of trouble.

"He doesn't love you," he called after her. "Has he said it? Has he ever actually said the words?"

She shook her head and did her best to ignore him. What a creep. But as she spotted Rafiq at the edge of the crowd and saw him smile, she realized Eric was right about one thing. Rafiq had never actually said he loved her.

Rafiq sat on the deck off the bedroom and listened as Kiley told their dog all about her evening.

"I can see that in addition to learning about the history of Lucia-Serrat and the protocol of being a princess, I'm going to need some dance lessons. I think I stepped on a lot of toes tonight, which can't be good. You want to learn to dance with me?"

Fari yipped in agreement. Rafiq smiled as he thought of the tiny puppy twirling around a ballroom.

Kiley stepped out onto the deck and plopped down next to him. She'd changed out of her ball gown and into a silk robe. Her makeup was gone, as was her jewelry. She looked young and fresh and very beautiful. But her eyes were troubled and he wanted to know why.

"You are still angry with me," he said.

"What?" She picked up Fari and set the dog on her lap. "Of course not. Why would I be mad?"

"Because of our conversation before."

"You mean when you were being unreasonable and stubborn? I'm sure I don't know what you're talking about." She leaned back in her chair. "I think you're wrong. I think it's important for you to let go of the past and meet your father as the man he is today. If you could simply walk away from him and wanted to do that, I would support it, but that's not the plan. You're moving back to the island where the two of you will work in close proximity. I can't imagine that going well if you can't get the past behind you where it belongs."

He liked that she held to her opinion even if he didn't agree with it. "Anything else?" he asked.

She shrugged. "You're not going to listen to me, which I accept but it makes me think you're not as bright as you look."

"So you insult me now?"

"I don't mean to, but it *is* a happy by-product of our conversation. I also know I can't make you do anything about your father. You're a grown-up and much bigger than me, so force is out of the question. I hope you'll deal with it, but if you won't, I'm going to try to let it go."

"Very wise. So what happened to upset you?" he asked. "Was it your conversation with Eric?"

She didn't act surprised that he knew about that. "I figured you saw us. What is it about that guy, always showing up everywhere? It's creepy."

Rafiq was less interested in that than the reason she was unhappy. "What did he say?"

"Nothing important. I just wish…" She looked at him. "Do you love me?"

He'd known they would get to that question eventually. He reached for her hand. "I have chosen you to be my wife, Kiley. I wish to marry you and have children with you. I ask you to join me as we rule over my country. You will be much beloved by my people."

She continued to study his face. "I get all that, but you didn't answer the question. Do you love me?"

"Is that so important to know?"

"It is to me." Tears filled her eyes. "Can't you say the words?" she asked in a whisper.

Her pain burned him, but a lie would burn more. "There is more to a marriage than love. There is respect, passion, caring. I will be true to you. I will treat you with respect and be there for our children. Isn't that enough?"

A single tear rolled down her cheek. Fari whined, as if sensing the tension between them.

"Rafiq, please. You must love me a little."

He rebelled against her attempts to weaken him. "How many times have we been together?" he asked, his voice more harsh than he would have liked. "How many times have I claimed you in the past few weeks?"

"I don't know. What does that have to do with anything? You can't seriously be equating sex with love. They're not the same at all."

"Are you on any birth control?"

There was little light on the deck and yet he saw the color drain from her face. Her eyes widened as she reached down to touch her stomach.

"You think I'm pregnant."

"I believe it is very likely."

She shrank from him. "Is that all this is about? A child? Are you s-saying you don't care about me at all?"

"I'm saying I want to marry you, Kiley. I want to be the father of your children. Isn't that enough?"

She stood, taking the puppy with her and walked toward the bedroom. At the French door, she looked back at him.

"It's not enough. It will never be enough. How could you think I would settle for that?"

Chapter Fifteen

Kiley was up before dawn the next morning. She'd barely been able to sleep at all. Her mind whirled with too many questions and possibilities, but nothing could be answered until she knew the truth.

So shortly after sunrise, she rose and dressed and made her way to the garage. Twenty minutes later she'd driven to the twenty-four-hour drugstore and bought a home pregnancy test. As she drove back to Rafiq's house, she wondered why she hadn't thought it could happen to her.

It's not as if she were an idiot. She knew how babies were made, and she and Rafiq had been doing that a lot lately. Condoms helped, but they also failed. But getting pregnant had never been a reality for her. She'd gone on The Pill six months ago so she wouldn't have to worry after she and Eric got married, but she'd had a bad reaction and had been forced to go off it. She'd discussed other options with her doctor yet hadn't acted on any of them. In truth, she'd wanted to get pregnant quickly and start her family.

But not like this, she thought as she pulled into the garage and sat in the car. Not when she'd just found out that Rafiq didn't love her, that he'd only proposed to her because he thought she was pregnant.

What if she was? She knew enough about the laws of Lucia-Serrat to know that the child of a member of the royal family could not be taken out of the country without permission from both the biological parent and the Crown Prince. As neither Rafiq nor Prince Nasri were likely to agree to that, she was well and truly stuck. Unlike Rafiq's mother, she would never turn her back on her child.

Tears burned in her eyes. She blinked them away. She'd done enough crying in the night, weeping silently as Rafiq had slept beside her. Pain had ripped through her and a sense of betrayal so deep, she knew she would bear the scars forever.

She'd loved him with every fiber of her being, and he hadn't loved her back. The truth couldn't be ignored or wished away.

Nearly as bad, she'd been so *sure* that he was the one. How could she have been wrong twice in a row? Why did she seem destined to fall for men who would lie to her?

She didn't have an answer and she couldn't stay in the car forever. After picking up the small bag from the drugstore, she made her way into the house and quietly walked down the hall to the bedroom.

For the first time since moving in with him, she wished she had her own room. She wanted space and privacy. She supposed she could move back to her own apartment. If she wasn't pregnant, she would. She would take some time and figure out what to do. Unlike her feelings for Eric, which had died over time, she loved Rafiq with an intensity that couldn't be described. She didn't think she could simply walk away from him forever.

He had to care, she told herself as she paused outside the bedroom door. He couldn't have made her so happy if he didn't. There had to be something between them, something he was unwilling to acknowledge. After his past was he unable to admit to any softer feelings?

She didn't have any answers, and right now what she most needed to know was whether or not she was carrying his child.

She walked into the bedroom and was surprised to find the bed empty. The bathroom door opened, and Rafiq stepped out. He'd already showered and dressed.

"You were up early," he said, his dark eyes giving nothing away.

"I couldn't sleep."

He glanced at the bag she held. "A pregnancy test?" he asked.

She nodded. "Then we'll both know."

"I'll wait."

She crossed to the bathroom, then stopped and looked at him.

"Is that why you proposed?" she asked. "Because you thought I might be pregnant? What if I'm not? Do you care about me even a little? Is any of this about me?"

"What do you want to know?" he asked. "You came to me, Kiley. You asked to be my mistress. I did not seek you out."

"I know." She squeezed her eyes shut, then opened them. "This was all my doing. You didn't force me. I thought I was tough. I wanted Eric punished and you were the best way I knew to do that. After a while I figured out I wasn't as interested in revenge as being with you."

She thought about the arguments she'd had with Eric. How he'd pressed her to admit there was something between her and her boss.

"He used to claim I had a thing for you and I always told him I didn't. Looking back at how quickly I fell for you, maybe he was right. Maybe he saw something I couldn't see. I mean, what was I thinking? Asking to be your mistress? It's crazy. You're right, you didn't force me to do anything. Not even to fall in love with you."

She paused, hoping he would say something to comfort her, but he didn't. There was only the quiet sound of her breathing.

She wanted to ask if he could ever come to love her, if she mattered at all, but she was afraid of the answer.

Ten minutes later she stared at the plastic stick and knew that her life had changed forever. There would be no going back to her old world, no moving out of Rafiq's house. She was bound to him as much as if they were chained together.

She washed her hands and dried them, then stepped out of the bathroom and faced him. "I'm pregnant," she whispered.

Rafiq heard the words but didn't believe them at first. He'd known it was possible, but to have it confirmed surprised him. He would have thought fate would give Kiley a chance to escape.

He didn't want her to go, he acknowledged, if only to himself. But without the baby, he had no other means to keep her.

She would be a good mother. She would care for their child, perhaps even love it. He would be there, as well, to make sure his son or daughter knew that there was a safe place to grow up. He knew all the things he had missed in his own childhood. Those mistakes would now be undone.

"I am pleased," he said.

"Really? I wouldn't think you were interested in a child. Will you love it? Will your baby matter?"

"Our children will be my world."

She leaned against the door frame and wiped the single tear that spilled out of one eye. "That's not the same. You have to be willing to give up your heart. You have to love children with all that you have, no matter what."

"As you will do," he said, stepping toward her and touching her chin. "Be happy. You said you always wanted to be a wife and mother. I am offering you that. You will be my princess and you will want for nothing. Our children will have untold opportunities to see the world, to grow strong. I will be there for you, all the days of my life. I will honor you. I will never betray you or be unfaithful or cruel. Is that not enough?"

She looked at him, her blue eyes damp with unshed tears. "There is a particular cruelty in not loving your wife," she said. "The kind that eats away at the soul."

She could be stubborn, but he'd always known that. "We will travel. See things, do things."

"You can't buy me, Rafiq. I'm not like your other women, remember? I'm not interested in pretty things."

"But you carry my child."

"That I do. Already I feel the chains tightening around my wrist."

"You're being overly dramatic. We will be married and you will be happy."

She stared at him. "No."

How like a woman. "Your refusal to accept happiness is your own decision."

"You misunderstand me. I'm not saying I won't be happy, I'm saying I won't marry you."

Disbelief held him in place. Otherwise he would have gone to her. To do what, he couldn't say. "You have no choice."

"Actually, I do. I might not know much about Lucia-Serrat, but I'm pretty sure there isn't a law that allows you to marry a woman against her will. Which means you can't make it happen without my agreement and I won't agree." She swallowed and wiped away tears. "I won't marry someone who doesn't love me."

This wasn't right, he thought. How dare she defy him? "You will not be able to take my child from me."

"I know that. I haven't figured it all out yet, but I do know that I'm not going to marry you. And aside from convincing me you're in love with me, there's nothing you can do to change my mind."

Rafiq battled fury for the next two days. While Kiley didn't labor over the topic, he sensed her determination. And try as he might, he couldn't seem to come up with any words that would convince her to see his side of things.

The prince and Phoebe seemed to sense the disquiet, for they spent much of that time touring the area, as if they wanted to avoid the house.

If Rafiq could have avoided it, he would. He hated that Kiley was so withdrawn. He missed her laughter, her pleasure in his company. In truth, he understood her need to stand firm on this issue. Unfortunately her principles brought her in direct opposition to his wishes. And he would win this battle, one way or the other.

"Aren't you going to the office?"

He looked up from his desk at the house and saw Kiley standing in the doorway. As always, the sight of her brought him gladness, followed by intense anger at her determination to be difficult.

"Eventually. I wish this resolved, first."

She stepped into the room. "You probably shouldn't wait that long. There are things you need to take care of."

"You won't marry me but still you worry about my work?"

She shrugged. "One has nothing to do with the other. Not marrying you doesn't make me care any less. It doesn't make me not love you."

She moved forward until she stood behind the chair in front of his desk. "I've been trying to figure out what's wrong," she said quietly, her voice filled with pain. "I have given my heart to you so completely that it's impossible for me to believe you don't want to do the same. You have all the symptoms of the condition, and yet you claim not to love me. And then I remember your past. What happened with your parents. Is that it,

Rafiq? Were you hurt too many times as a child to believe in love?"

The question made him sound weak and he refused
to answer. "My reasons aren't important."

"They are to me. I comfort myself with the fact that
this isn't personal. You wouldn't love anyone, would
you? What are you afraid of?"

He glared at her. "I have no fear."

"You have something. Is it being hurt? Is it that I'll
go away? Because I won't. I don't want to. I'm not your
parents. If you don't believe me, look to my family, at
what I've been taught. My parents are as much in love
today as when they were married. My sisters have wonderful relationships. I made a mistake with Eric, but
even there I was loyal. He was the one who betrayed me."

Her words hurt him as much as if she'd attacked him
with a knife. "You will marry me."

"No. Not until you can admit you love me. Because
that's the irony of the situation. I think you do. I think
I matter more than anyone has ever mattered and you're
terrified of that. You're afraid of being hurt and abandoned. There's nothing I can say or do to convince you
otherwise, so this is all about a step of faith. Are you
willing to take it?"

He stood. "Do not presume to know my mind," he
told her coldly.

Her shoulders slumped. "Right. Because pride matters the most. Don't you get tired of always being right
but always being alone?"

She turned and left the room. Silence surrounded
him, pressed down on him, gutted him and he could not
say why.

* * *

Rafiq transferred most of his operation to the house. He told himself it was so that he could spend time with his father and Phoebe, but in truth it was so he could keep an eye on Kiley. How long would she stay? When would she bolt for freedom?

That had to be her plan and he couldn't let her escape with his child.

He reviewed the oil reserve reports, stopping only when his father walked into the study and took a seat.

"Good news?" Nasri asked, nodding at the papers.

"Yes. The reserves are much larger than we calculated at first. Unlike other parts of the world, we will have oil into the next century."

"That bodes well for our future economy," the prince said. He leaned back in the leather chair and studied his son. "Do you see much of your mother these days?"

Rafiq shook his head and tried not to show his surprise at the question. "I have spoken with her twice in the past two months, but before that it was nearly a year since our paths crossed."

"So you don't have regular contact with her?"

"No. There is no reason."

The prince shrugged. "She *is* your mother."

"She and I have a biological connection, but little else."

"She was never warm or maternal," Prince Nasri said. "But she was very beautiful. I remember the first time I saw her. She was filming a scene on the beach. I was taken with her beauty. She was older by five years. When I was seventeen, that made her seem a woman of the world." He smiled. "I wanted her to be my first."

Rafiq hadn't known that, and frankly he could have

gone a long time without hearing the information. He and his father weren't very close, but that didn't mean he was comfortable discussing the man's sex life with Rafiq's mother.

"I didn't love her," Nasri continued. "Love wasn't important to me. Fortunately she didn't love me, either, so neither of us was hurt. Although there was an injured party."

He paused significantly. Rafiq knew his father meant him, but refused to say anything.

"It was never my intention to wound you," the prince said.

"I survived and grew up," Rafiq told him. "Unless you have complaints about my work?"

"Not at all. You do your duties extremely well. Somehow you managed to raise yourself with the help of a few nannies and tutors. You should be proud."

Rafiq shifted in his chair. "I find no cause for pride."

"I'm sure that is true, but still I have regrets. I think about what you went through and how I should have been there. I was but a child myself, yet I find that excuse has less and less meaning as I get older."

If Rafiq didn't know it wasn't possible, he would swear that his father had been speaking with Kiley. She had been pushing for a reconciliation. Instead it had come from an unlikely source. At what point should he explain that none of this was necessary?

"The past is just that. Over," Rafiq said. "I appreciate your worry on my behalf, but it doesn't matter now."

"I think it does. I am worried about your relationship with Kiley."

He bristled. "That is not your concern."

"You are my son. That makes it my concern. Phoebe and I noticed that you both seem less happy than when we arrived."

"It is nothing."

Prince Nasri didn't respond. Silence filled the room. At last Rafiq spoke.

"She has refused to marry me, despite the fact that she carries my child. While I offer her the world, she wants only a declaration of love."

"Which you will not give her," the prince said. "Because you do not believe."

Rafiq wanted to hurry from the room. He didn't like this conversation.

Nasri leaned toward him. "My son, I cannot tell you how sorry I am. It is my fault you resist Kiley's precious gift. You haven't seen much love in your life and that is because of me. I wasn't there. I didn't show you what—"

Rafiq rose. "Do you think any of this matters to me?"

"It should."

"No. She will marry me. With the child, she has no choice."

The prince stood and faced him. "Why won't you trust her? Why won't you let her prove herself?"

Because no one had ever loved him enough to stay.

Rafiq didn't speak the words, but they reverberated inside his brain. All his life people had left. He had learned not to care, not to let them close enough so that their disappearance was more than a sting. So it was with Kiley. He would keep her at arm's length, but he *would* keep her.

Without saying anything more, he walked out of the room and left his father. There was a solution, he thought. And he would find it.

Chapter Sixteen

Kiley was thinking that this wasn't the best week she'd ever had. Everything had started out with such promise. How had she ended up sad and afraid? Afraid because she didn't know how to convince Rafiq that caring about her was safe.

"May I join you?"

She looked up and saw Phoebe had strolled onto the deck. "Thank you, yes," Kiley told her. "I'm tired of my own company."

Rafiq's stepmother stretched out on the lounge chair and sighed. "I'm enjoying my time here. At home there are a thousand-and-one things that need my attention. Not to mention how much the girls keep me busy. But here there is only family and a chance to relax."

"I'm glad you're enjoying yourself."

Phoebe turned to look at her. "You are not, I fear. Nasri and I know about your situation with Rafiq."

Kiley winced. "Tell me you didn't hear us fighting."

"Of course not. You've been most discreet. But the mood changed, and then Rafiq spoke with his father."

"On purpose?" Kiley asked before she could stop herself. "Sorry. I just didn't think they talked about anything personal."

"They don't. Nasri never knows what to say, although he would rather slice off his arm than admit it. The fear of saying the wrong thing causes him to be critical. Rafiq expects the worst and jumps on any misstep. I have tried, but they are both stubborn. Still, they spoke. I don't think the wounds are healed, but they are acknowledged."

"I wish Rafiq could get along with his father. He needs that connection." He needed a place to call home, she thought. "He's so good with me, and I know he'll be good with our baby. It's just…" She winced. "You knew about the baby, didn't you?"

Phoebe smiled. "Yes. That's one of the reasons I wanted to talk to you." She glanced back toward the open door, then lowered her voice. "Kiley, I can help you."

"How? No offense, but I have trouble believing you're going to click your fingers and have Rafiq falling at my feet."

"Unfortunately, no. But I can help you get away."

Kiley shifted Fari off her lap and sat up in the lounge chair. "I don't understand. You want me to leave?"

"Of course not. It's just…I know you're unhappy and I'm very clear on the law of the land. Your child will have to be raised on Lucia-Serrat. Your choice is to leave the child or live on the island and deal with Rafiq."

"I figured that part out." It was like being between a rock and a hard place. "I'll be moving to the island."

"You don't have to." Phoebe stared at her intently. "I can take you to a place where Rafiq will never find you. There you can raise your child alone. Without him." Phoebe sighed. "I don't like making this offer, but as a mother, I understand how much you love your baby. You would do anything to keep him or her close. I wanted you to know this was an option."

Kiley wasn't sure she could have been more surprised if Phoebe had sprouted wings. "That's not possible."

"It is. It will take time, but it can be done."

Go away? Leave Rafiq?

"I would have liked your offer a lot better if you'd come to me with a way to make Rafiq fall in love with me." She sighed. "Actually, I don't think I need help with that. I think he does love me, but he won't admit it. Maybe he doesn't know what love feels like and he can't recognize it. A remote possibility but one I hold out hope for. I think it's more likely that he's simply not willing to trust me."

Kiley petted Fari. "I wish I knew how to let him know I'm not going to abandon him. Not ever."

"That requires a step of faith."

"I don't think Rafiq is very interested in faith right now." Kiley looked at Phoebe. "Thanks for the offer, but no."

"Don't you want to think about it?" Phoebe asked.

"I don't need to. I love Rafiq and I love his baby. I'm not turning my back on either one. I have no idea how I'm going to make this all work out, but I'll come up with a plan."

"I would be most interested to hear it," Rafiq said as he stepped onto the balcony.

His timely arrival and Phoebe's look of guilt was all Kiley needed. She grabbed Fari, stood and faced her former fiancé.

"You set me up," she said, her voice shaking with fury. She wanted to scream and hit and punish him for doing this to her. "How dare you?"

"I am Prince Rafiq of—"

"No one here gives a crap," she told him, glaring at him and wishing she was big enough to beat some sense into him. "It's not enough that you tricked me into an engagement you didn't mean, but now you're using people I like and trust to set me up?"

"I'm sorry," Phoebe murmured.

"I know," Kiley said, aware that it would be a while before she could forgive the other woman. "That's not the point." She turned back to Rafiq. "What was the purpose? What were you looking for?"

"The truth."

"What? Did you want to know if I was like your mother? You already have that answer. What other information do you need? Tell me and I'll give it to you." She squared her shoulders. "Which would have made you feel more like a man? Having me choose you or our child? I'm sorry, but you're not going to get that question answered. I refuse to choose and you can't make me."

She started toward him, then pushed past him and walked into the living room. Once there, she faced him again.

"This was a big mistake, Rafiq, because now I think less of you. You hurt me and you have no right to do that."

"I need to know."

"What? What is missing? You can keep trying to trip me up, but it's not going to work. I love you. There are no strings, no games, and only one expectation, which is that you'll love me back. Why is that so hard for you to understand?"

Rafiq watched her walk away. Phoebe came up beside him.

"That was a mistake," she said. "I warned you. I didn't want to do it and I feel horrible for being a part of your ridiculous plan. Don't ask me to do something like that again."

He felt her anger, but it was nothing when compared with Kiley's. He felt uncomfortable and didn't know why. He had the right to do as he pleased.

"I must be sure," he said, as much to himself as to Phoebe.

"Of what? That her love is real? Let me give you a word of advice. Love stretched too far can break. And then what will you have?" Phoebe shook her head. "Is that what this is all about? Are you trying to make her leave so you are once again right? Who wins then?"

She left and he was alone. Below, on the beach, several children played in the surf. There were teenagers and couples, families and an old man reading the newspaper. Life continued and yet he felt trapped in silence. As if he was out of step with all of it.

He wanted to believe. He wanted to trust. But how?

He sank onto the chair Kiley had vacated and closed his eyes. Her sentences replayed in his mind. Her question asking which would make him feel more like a man—her choosing him or their child.

He didn't want to feel more like a man, he told himself. He wanted...

"I wish Rafiq could get along with his father. He needs that connection."

Kiley's words were as real as if she'd just spoken them again. She worried about him. She wanted him to be happy. She wanted him to have a family beyond just her.

He knew why. He knew what her parents meant to her, and she wanted the same thing for him. She wanted him to have more. To be more. He knew in his head that she was all he could want, but in his heart...

Fari walked onto the deck. She trotted to the edge and looked over at two boys playing with a Frisbee. Her entire body quivered with excitement as she silently pleaded to be included.

Rafiq stood and walked toward the puppy. She was enthusiastic and foolish. If she didn't pay attention—

It happened so quickly. The Frisbee sailed too close to the deck and Fari grabbed for it. She slipped easily through the railing and nearly caught the toy, just as gravity caught her. Rafiq lunged for her and barely snagged the scruff of her neck.

Man and dog stared at each other. Fari twisted her head and licked his arm as she waited for him to pull her to safety. It never occurred to her he wouldn't. He could drop her and she would fall nearly twenty feet. She could be injured or killed and it never crossed her tiny puppy mind.

It was because she didn't know better, he told himself, even as he acknowledged her instinctive faith in him. She had never fallen before and he had never rescued her, but it didn't occur to her that he wouldn't.

He pulled her up to safety and set her on his lap.

"Just as well," he muttered to the dog. "Kiley adores you. She wouldn't want anything to happen to you."

He thought about how she fussed over the dog, talking to her, playing with her, caring for her. How much more would she love their child? How much more would she care and fuss and worry?

There were so many people in her life and yet she managed to love them all. How big was her heart? Big enough to hold him?

He set Fari down and she scampered out of the room, yipping for Kiley as she went. He stood and faced the same doorway. A single step of faith. That was all she wanted from him.

In his past were too many people who had let down a child desperately in need of affection. In his future...who could say? But he knew what was offered.

He walked after Fari, following the sound of her barking. But instead of settling in one place, she circled through the rooms, her barks growing more frantic as she was unable to find Kiley.

Rafiq searched, as well. He collected the little dog and did his best to reassure her, but she wasn't comforted. When he couldn't find Kiley anywhere, neither was he.

She was gone along with Phoebe and his father. Had they taken her away? Was she even now being whisked to a location he would never find?

"Kiley!" he yelled as he hurried toward the garage and jerked open the door. Her car was still there, but what did that symbolize? She'd never been overly impressed by what his money could buy.

He raced to their bedroom and threw open the closet doors. All her clothes were still there. He stopped and breathed in the scent of her perfume. If her clothes were still here, then—

The front door slammed. He ran toward the sound, then came to a stop when he saw her walking through the living room.

"Where have you been?" he asked more harshly than he would have liked.

"Watering the plants on the front porch. They were looking a little dry. Your parents have gone out to a movie. Your father said it's been years since he's been in a real movie theater. He's looking forward to the popcorn."

She smiled as she spoke, but her eyes were still sad. He wanted to go to her and offer comfort, but he was the problem.

Fari squirmed. He set her down and she raced over to Kiley who picked her up.

"What have you been getting yourself into?" Kiley asked. "Something bad. I can tell."

"You didn't leave."

Kiley looked at him. "What?"

"I thought you'd left. I couldn't find you and I thought…"

She sighed heavily. "I wish I could crawl into your brain and do a little work there. I'm not leaving. I don't know how many times I have to tell you that. I'm angry. I think you're a clueless jerk, but I'm not going anywhere."

She cuddled the dog as she looked at him. "I think you love me and that's what keeps me hanging on. I think somewhere deep in the cloudy brain of yours is a seed of faith, and I'm going to figure out how to get to it."

"Are you going to marry me?"

"Eventually. When you stop being stupid."

He narrowed his gaze. "You toss your insults around very freely."

She actually smiled. "So what are you going to do about it? Punish me? I'm the mother of your child and the woman you want to marry. You're going to fall all over yourself to treat me with reverence and respect. You're going to cater to my every wish, even the silly ones." Her smile faded. "So I'm not scared of you and I'm not leaving. Somehow we're going to become a family."

"But you won't marry me."

She stared at him. "Earth to Rafiq. Could we get some new material here?"

"So you're willing to give up being my wife and a princess. You'll have my child outside of marriage, return to Lucia-Serrat with me and live in the palace as the mother of my child, but you won't be my wife."

She considered for a moment, then nodded. "That about sums it up."

She spoke the truth. He could feel it in her words and the steadiness of her gaze. Not once in all the time he'd known her had she ever lied. She'd never even stretched the truth. She acted with integrity and honored her commitments. She *loved*.

He moved closer but didn't touch her. "I learned to write very early," he told her. "My tutors marveled at my ability to grasp the concept. What they didn't know is that I had been waiting since I realized what writing was. I knew that if I could get a letter to my mother, if I could explain that I was alone, that I loved and needed her, she would come and be with me."

Kiley felt her heart crumble. As Rafiq spoke, she pictured the lonely little boy, abandoned by his parents, growing up in the company of the palace staff. Somehow this proud, strong man had survived, had *thrived*.

"What happened?" she asked, already suspecting the answer.

"It took her several months to write me back, and when she did, she told me to ask my father for a pony. She said he was plenty rich and would give it to me."

Kiley set Fari on the floor, then rushed toward Rafiq and wrapped her arms around him. "I'm so sorry," she whispered. "I wish I could go back in time and beat up both your parents. Or at the very least, find you and take care of you myself."

He kissed the top of her head, then touched her chin so that she looked at him. "I do not."

"Why?"

"Because I would rather have you as my wife today than as my babysitter twenty-five years ago."

"But the little boy needed so much love."

"So does the man."

She blinked. "Excuse me?"

"This man needs your love with a desperation he cannot describe." He stroked her cheeks with his thumbs, then kissed her mouth. "I need you, Kiley. I need you to love me, to keep loving me. I need you to show me what is possible. What we can have together. What we can be."

"Rafiq."

Her chest tightened until it was difficult to breathe. Was this the first crack in the shell? A way to get through to him? Oh, please, let it be so.

His dark eyes stared into hers. "All my life I've held myself back from the people closest to me. No one was allowed to be in a position to hurt me again."

"I would never do that," she breathed.

"I know."

"I love you."

He gazed at her for a long time, then kissed her again. "I know," he said at last.

Hope burst forth and made her want to laugh with happiness. "You believe me? You believe that love is possible?"

"With you."

Was it wrong to want it all? "Could you love me?"

In a movement that stunned her, in a moment she would treasure for the rest of her life, Kiley watched as Prince Rafiq of Lucia-Serrat fell to his knees. He grasped her around her thighs and buried his face in her stomach. She felt the tension in his body, the battle that raged.

How she ached for him, for *them*. If only he could—

"I love you," he said, his voice cracking with emotion. "Dear God, I love you, Kiley."

She dropped next to him and pulled him close. He held on to her as if he would never let her go.

"I love you, too," she whispered into his ear. "I think longer than I should have. Perhaps since I first met you, which, given my former engagement, is fairly tacky."

He raised his head and smiled at her. The powerful emotions in his eyes, the love there, was so bright it nearly blinded her.

"Imagine if you hadn't caught Eric cheating," he said.

"No. I don't want to do that. I don't want to imagine any future without you."

"Nor do I." He touched his chest. "I feel a release. The walls are crumbling."

Tears filled her eyes, but for the first time in days, they were happy ones. She clung to him and rested her head on his shoulder. He wrapped his arms around her.

"Just hold me," she whispered. "I never want to let go."

"Eventually you will have to. Fari will need to be walked and fed. We will get hungry ourselves."

She straightened and shoved him back. "We're having a moment here. It's not every day the future Crown Prince of Lucia-Serrat tells me he loves me."

He leaned in and brushed his lips against hers. "Yes, it is," he murmured. "So many times a day, you will grow tired of hearing it."

She was so happy, she could have floated. "That's not going to happen." She grinned. "So I guess the wedding's back on."

"No."

"What?"

"Don't marry me," he told her. "Wait until I have proved myself."

"What?" she repeated. "Are you crazy?"

"A little. I want you to be sure. I want you to know that I mean what I say. That this isn't a trick to get you to the altar."

She stood up and put her hands on her hips. "There's going to be a wedding when we planned."

"No, Kiley. My way is better."

She raised her eyes to the heavens. "I'm going to have to kill him. I see that now and I apologize in advance. I'll probably go to prison but it will be worth it."

He stood and picked her up in his arms. "Before you

get out the swords or however it is you plan to do me in, I want to make love with you several thousand times."

She settled an arm around his neck and relaxed against him. "Okay, but just so we're clear, there's going to be a wedding."

"We shall see."

Epilogue

There was a wedding and it was held on the originally scheduled date in the beautiful church on the island of Lucia-Serrat. The fall weather was perfect, warm and sunny during the day and cool and clear at night.

The royal families from both El Bahar and Bahania attended, and there were whispers that the bride of the king of El Bahar, who was also the mother of the Prince of Thieves, was with child. At her age, that was both a miracle and a scandal. King Givon and Queen Cala weren't talking, but their glow of happiness gave them away.

Kiley and Rafiq attended many parties in their honor. She found herself meeting princes and princesses she had only read about in magazines. But all were gracious and accepting. The crown prince of El Bahar bemoaned the beauty of his now-teenage stepdaughter and he was furious to find her flirting with the youngest brother of Princess Billie of Bahania.

The wife of the Prince of Thieves offered an incredible Ming dynasty vase collection as a wedding gift without being clear on where it had come from. Princess Dora of El Bahar exchanged phone numbers with Princess Daphne of Bahania, and Kiley felt as if she'd fallen into the middle of a very exciting, very royal soap opera.

Kiley could have been intimidated by her new friends and relatives, but when she saw the light of love in the men's eyes, the same love she saw in Rafiq's, she knew there was nothing to fear. These strong, powerful kings and princes weren't all that different from other men. They worked, they worried, they loved. The desert blood that flowed through their bodies made them loyal unto death, and she couldn't wait to be a part of all that.

On the morning of her wedding, her sisters and her mother helped her into her beautiful white gown. There were buttons to fasten, shoes to slip into and a tiara to anchor to her short hair. Rafiq had sent sapphires to match her eyes, rubies to represent his heart and a diamond necklace to bind them together always.

At last it was time. Ann and Heather walked down the aisle first, then Kiley linked arms with her father and they moved toward the entrance to the church.

"You sure about this?" her father joked. "We could still make a run for it."

She laughed. "I love you, Daddy. I'll miss you and mom so much, but this is where I belong."

He kissed her cheek. "I always knew you were a princess, honey. I just didn't know you were going to get a crown to go with it."

The tall doors to the church opened, and Kiley and her father stepped inside.

There were nearly five hundred guests in attendance. Music swelled to the high rafters, and sunlight poured through the stained-glass windows. But Kiley didn't see any of it. For her there was only one person there. A man who waited, who loved her.

Rafiq stood at the end of the long aisle, and she had to remind herself to walk slowly. A bride racing to her groom would give the press too much to talk about.

So she took small steps and smiled at the guests, but in her heart she waited to be with her prince. And when she finally stood next to him, he took her hands and gazed at her.

"I'm going to be saying it for all the world to hear," he told her quietly, "but I want to say it to you first. I love you, Kiley."

"I love you, too." She smiled. "I was thinking about how all this started. With that very unusual question."

He grinned. "As it happens, I'm not looking for a mistress. I'm looking for a wife. Interested?"

"Oh, yeah."

The minister cleared his throat. "The wedding?"

Rafiq squeezed her fingers. "Sure. Let's do that."

The old man smiled, then spoke in a solemn voice. "Dearly beloved…"

Don't miss the newest continuity from
Silhouette Special Edition,
THE FAMILY BUSINESS
launching in January 2006 with
PRODIGAL SON
by Susan Mallery.
And now, turn the page for a sneak peek
at Susan's new novel
DELICIOUS
Available from HQN Books in February 2006.

Chapter One

Penny Jackson knew that it was probably wrong of her to be so excited to see her ex-husband come crawling back, but she was willing to live with the character flaw.

"You know he's going to want to hire you," her friend Naomi said.

"Oh, yeah. The sweet smell of validation." Penny leaned back in her chair and considered the possibilities. "I want him to beg. Not in a vicious, I-hate-your-guts way, but more as a…"

"Show of support for divorced women everywhere?" Naomi asked.

Penny laughed. "Exactly. I suppose that makes me petty and small."

"Maybe, but you're looking especially fabulous today, if that helps."

"A little." Penny smoothed the front of her loose sweater and glanced at the clock. "We're meeting for lunch downtown. A neutral location—no memories, good or bad."

"Stay away from the good ones," Naomi warned her. "You always were a sucker where Cal was concerned."

"That was so three years ago. I'm completely over him. I've moved on."

"Right." Naomi didn't look convinced. "Don't think about how great he looks in his clothes, or out of them. Instead remember how he broke your heart, lied about wanting children and trampled your fragile dreams."

Easy enough, Penny thought, a flicker of annoyance muscling in on her good mood.

Nearly as bad, four years ago she'd applied for a job as a cook in Buchanan's, one of Cal's family's restaurants. The job had been strictly entry level—she would have been in charge of salads. There had been ten other applicants. Worried she wouldn't make the cut, Penny had asked her then husband to put in a good word for her with his grandmother. He'd refused and she hadn't gotten the job.

"This time the job is coming to me," Penny said. "I intend to take advantage of that. And him. In a strictly business way, of course."

"Of course," Naomi echoed, not sounding the least bit convinced. "He's trouble for you. Always has been. Be careful."

Penny stood and reached for her purse. "When am I not?"

"Ask for lots of money."

"I promise."

"Don't think about having sex with him."

Penny laughed. "Oh, please. That isn't an issue. You'll see."

Penny arrived early, then stayed in her car until five minutes after the appointed time. A small, possibly insignificant power play on her part, but she figured she'd earned it.

She walked into the quiet, leather and linen bistro. Before she could approach the hostess, she saw Cal standing by a booth in the back. They might have friends in common, and live in the same city, but since she'd done her darnedest to avoid close proximity to him, they never ran into each other. This lunch was going to change that.

"Hi," she said with a breezy smile.

"Penny." He looked her over, then motioned to the other side of the booth. "Thanks for joining me."

"How could I refuse? You wouldn't say much over the phone, which made me curious." She slid onto the seat.

Cal looked good. Tall, muscled, the same soulful eyes she remembered. Just sitting across from him caused her body to remember what it had been like back when things had been good and they'd been unable to keep their hands off each other. Not that she was interested in him in that way. She'd learned her lesson.

Plus, she couldn't forgive the fact that in the three years they'd been apart, he hadn't had the common courtesy to get fat or wrinkled. Nope, he was gorgeous—which was just like a man.

Still, he needed her help. Oh, yeah, that part was very cool. While they'd been married, the message had been she wasn't good enough. Now he wanted her to save the day…or the restaurant, in this case. While she planned to say yes eventually, she was going to enjoy every second of making him beg.

"The Waterfront is in trouble," he said, then paused as the waitress came by to take their order.

When the woman left, Penny leaned back in the tufted seat of the booth and smiled. "I'd heard it was more than trouble. I'd heard the place was done for. Hemorrhaging customers and money."

She blinked, going for an innocent expression. No doubt Cal would see through her attempt and want to strangle her. Verbally, at least. But he couldn't. Because he *needed* her. Was, in fact, desperate for her help. How she loved that in a man. Especially in Cal.

"Things have been better," he admitted, looking as if he hated every second of the conversation.

"The Waterfront is the oldest restaurant in the infamous Buchanan Dynasty," she said cheerfully. "The flagship. Or it used to be. Now you have a reputation for bad food and worse service." She sipped her water. "At least, that's the word on the street."

"Thanks for the update."

His jaw tightened as he spoke. She could tell he was furious about this meeting. She had an idea of what he was thinking—of all the chefs in all of Seattle, why did it have to be her?

She didn't know, either, but sometimes a girl couldn't help catching a break.

"Your contract is up," he said.

She smiled. "Yes, it is."

"You're looking for a new position."

"Yes, I am."

"I'd like to hire you."

Five little words. Words that weren't significant on their own, but when joined together, could mean the world to someone. In this case, her.

"I've had other offers," Penny said calmly.

"Have you accepted any of them?"

"Not yet."

Cal was tall, about six-three, with dark hair. His face was all sculpted cheekbones and stubborn jaw, and his mouth frequently betrayed his mood. Right now it was thin and straight. He was so angry, he practically spouted steam. She'd never felt better.

"I'm here to offer you a five-year contract. You get complete control of the kitchen, the standard agreement." He named a salary that made her blink.

Penny took another sip of her water. In truth she didn't want just another job. She wanted her own place. But opening a restaurant took serious money, which she didn't have. Her choices were to take on more partners than she wanted or wait. She'd decided to wait.

Her plan was to spend the next three years putting away money, then open the restaurant of her dreams. So while a big salary was nice, it wasn't enough.

"Not interested," she said with a slight smile.

Cal's gaze narrowed. "What do you want? Aside from my head on a stick."

Her smile turned genuine. "I've never wanted that," she told him. "Well, not after the divorce was final. It's been three years, Cal. I've long since moved on. Haven't you?"

"Of course. Then why aren't you interested? It's a good job."

"I'm not looking for a job. I want an opportunity."

"Meaning?"

"More than the standard agreement. I want my name out front and complete creative control in back." She reached into the pocket of her jacket and pulled out a folded piece of paper. "I have a list."

Doing the right thing had always been a pain in the ass, Cal thought, as he took the sheet and unfolded it. This time was no different.

He scanned the list, then tossed it back to her. Penny didn't want an opportunity, she wanted his balls sautéed with garlic and a nice cream sauce.

"No," he said flatly, ignoring the way the afternoon sunlight brought out the different colors of red and brown in her auburn hair.

"Fine by me." She picked up the sheet and started to slide out of the booth. "Nice to see you, Cal. Good luck with the restaurant."

He reached across the table and grabbed her wrist. "Wait."

"But if we have nothing to talk about…"

She looked innocent enough, he thought, as he gazed into her big blue eyes, but he knew better than to believe the wide-eyed stare.

Penny could be convinced to take the job, otherwise she wouldn't have bothered with a meeting. Playing him for a fool wasn't her style. But that didn't mean she wouldn't enjoy making him beg.

Given their past, he supposed he'd earned it. So he would bargain with her, giving in where he had to. He would even have enjoyed the negotiation if only she wouldn't look so damn smug.

He rubbed his thumb across her wrist bone, knowing she would hate that. She'd always lamented about her large forearms, wrists and hands, claiming they were out of proportion with the rest of her body. He'd thought she was crazy to obsess about a flaw that didn't exist. Besides, she had chef's hands—scarred, nimble and strong. He'd always liked her hands, whether they were working on food in the kitchen or working on him in the bedroom.

"Not going to happen," he said, nodding his head at the paper and releasing his hold on her. "You know that, too. So where is the real list of demands?"

She grinned and eased back into the booth. "I heard you were desperate. I had to try."

"Not that desperate. What do you want?"

"Creative freedom on the menus, complete control over the back half of the store, my name on the menu, ownership of any specialty items I create, the right to refuse any general manager you try to stuff down my throat, four weeks vacation a year and ten percent of the profits."

The waitress appeared with their lunches. He'd ordered a burger, Penny a salad. But not just any salad. Their server laid out eight plates with various ingredients in front of Penny's bowl of four kinds of lettuce.

As he watched, she put olive oil, balsamic vinegar and ground pepper into a coffee cup, then squeezed in half a lemon. After whisking them with her fork, she dumped the diced, smoked chicken and feta onto her salad, then sniffed the candied pecans before adding them. She passed over walnuts, took only half of the tomato, added red onions instead of green and then put on her dressing. After tossing everything, she stacked the plates and took her first bite of lunch.

"How is it?" he asked.

"Good."

"Why do you bother eating out?"

"I don't usually."

She hadn't before, either. She'd been content to whip up something incredible in their kitchen, and he'd been happy to let her.

He returned his attention to her demands. He wouldn't give her what she wanted on general principle. Plus it was just plain bad business.

"You can have creative control over the menus and the back half of the store," he said. "Specialty items stay with the house."

Anything a chef created while in the employ of a restaurant was owned by that restaurant.

"I want to be able to take them with me when I go." She forked a piece of lettuce. "It's a deal breaker, Cal."

"You'll come up with something new there."

"The point is I don't want to create something wonderful and leave it in your family's less-than-capable hands." She narrowed her gaze. "Before you get all defensive, let me point out that five years ago, the Waterfront had a waiting list every single weekend."

"You can have your name on the menu," he said. "As executive chef."

He saw her stiffen. She'd never had that title before. It would mean something now.

"And three percent of the profits," he added.

"Eight."

"Four."

"Six."

"Five," he said. "But you don't get a say in the general manager."

"I have to work with him or her."

"And he or she has to work with you."

She grinned. "But I have a reputation of being nothing but sunshine and light in the workplace. You know that."

He'd heard she was a perfectionist and relentless in her quest for quality. She had also been called difficult, annoying and just plain brilliant.

"You can't dictate the GM," he said. "He's already been hired. At least in the short term."

She wrinkled her nose. "Who is it?"

"You'll find out later. Besides, the first guy's just coming in to do clean-up. Someone else will be hired in a few months. You can have a say on him or her."

Her eyebrows rose. "Interesting. A gunslinger coming in to clean up the town. I think I like that." She drew in a breath. "How about five percent of the profits, a three-year deal, I get some say in the next GM and I take my specialty items with me." She held up her hand. "But only to my own place, and you can keep them on the Waterfront menu as well."

He wasn't surprised she wanted to branch out on her own. Most good chefs did. Few had the capital or the management skills.

"Oh, and that salary you offered me before was fine," she said.

"Of course it was," he told her. "That assumed you didn't get this other stuff. How many are you bringing with you?"

"Two. My sous-chef and my assistant."

Chefs usually came with a small staff. As long as they worked well with the others in the kitchen, Cal didn't care.

"You'll never take the vacation," he said. At least she never had before.

"I want it," she said. "Just so we're clear, I *will* be using it."

He shrugged. "Not until we're up and running."

"I was thinking late summer. I'll have everything together by then."

Maybe. She hadn't seen the mess yet.

"Is that it?" he asked.

She considered for a second, then shrugged. "Get me the offer in writing. I'll look it over and then let you know if we have a deal."

"You'd never get this much anywhere else. Don't pretend you'll back out."

The smugness returned. "You never know, Cal. I want to hear what your competition puts on the table."

"I know who's interested. They'll never cut you in for that much of the profit."

"True enough, but their restaurants are successful. A smaller percentage of something is better than a big chunk of nothing."

"This could make you a star," he said. "People would notice."

"People already notice."

He wanted to tell her she wasn't all that special. That he could name five chefs who would do as good a job. The problem was—he couldn't. In the past three years, Penny had made a name for herself. He needed that to dig the Waterfront out of its hole.

"I'll have the agreement couriered over to your place tomorrow afternoon," he said.

She practically purred her contentment. "Good."

"You're enjoying this, aren't you?"

"Oh, yeah. I won't even mind working for you, because every time you piss me off, I'm going to remind you that you came looking for me. That you *needed* me."

Revenge. He suspected that. It annoyed him, but he respected it.

"Why are you doing this?" she asked as she picked up a pecan. "You got out of the family business years ago."

Back when they'd been married, he thought. He'd escaped, only to be dragged in again.

"Someone had to save the sinking ship," he said.

"Yes, but why you? You don't care about the family empire."

He threw twenty dollars on the table and slid out of the booth. "I'll need your answer within twenty-four hours of you getting the contract."

"You'll have it the following morning."

"Fair enough." He dropped a business card next to the money. "In case you need to get in touch with me."

He walked out of the restaurant and headed for the parking lot where he'd left his car. Penny was going to say yes. She would screw with him a little, but the deal was too good for her to pass up. If she pulled it off, if she made the Waterfront what it had once been, then in three years she would have more than enough capital to start her own place.

He would be gone long before that. He'd agreed to come in to temporarily get things up and running, but he had no desire to stay to the bitter end. His only concern was saving the sinking ship. Let someone else shine it up and take all the glory. He was only interested in getting out.

Penny walked into the Downtown Sports Bar and Grill a little after two in the afternoon. The lunch crowd had pretty much cleared out, although a few diehards sat watching the array of sports offered on various televisions around the place.

She headed directly for the bar and leaned against the polished wood. "Hi, Mandy. Is he in?" she asked the very-large-breasted blonde polishing glasses.

Mandy smiled. "Hi, Penny. Yeah. He's in his office. Want me to bring you anything?"

Caffeine, Penny thought, then shook her head. "I'm good."

She walked to the right of the bar, where a small alcove offered rest room choices, a pay phone and a door marked Employees. From there it was a short trip to Reid Buchanan's cluttered office.

He sat behind a desk as big as a full-size mattress, his feet up on the corner, the telephone cradled between his ear and his shoulder. When he saw her, he rolled his eyes, pointed at the phone, then waved her in.

"I know," he said as she wove her way around boxes he had yet to unpack. "It is an important event, and I'd like to be there, but I have a prior engagement. Maybe next time. Uh-huh. Sure. You, too."

He hung up the phone and groaned. "Some foreign government trade-show crap," he said.

"What did they want you to do?" she asked as she swept several folders off the only other chair in the office and sank onto the hard wooden seat. She dumped the folders onto his already piled desk.

"Not a clue. Show up. Smile for pictures. Maybe give a speech." He shrugged.

"How much were they willing to pay you?"

He dropped his feet to the floor and turned to face her. "Ten grand. It's not like I need the money. I hate all that. It's bogus. I used to play baseball and now I'm here. I've retired."

Just last year, Penny thought. With the start of the regular season just weeks away, Reid had to be missing his former life.

She poked at one of the piles on the desk, then glanced at him. "I distinctly remember you saying you wanted a desk big enough to have sex on. It was a very specific requirement when we went shopping for one. But if you keep it this messy, no one will be interested in getting naked on the very impressive surface."

He leaned back in his chair and grinned at her. "I don't need the desk to get 'em naked."

"So I've heard."

Reid Buchanan was legendary. Not just for his incredible career as a Major League pitcher, but for the way women adored him. Part of it was the Buchanan good looks and charm that all the brothers had. Part of it was Reid just plain loved women. All women. He didn't so much have a type as a gender. Former girlfriends ranged from the traditional models and actresses to Mother Earth tree huggers nearly a decade older than him. Smart, dumb, short, tall, skinny, curvy, he liked them all. And they liked him.

Penny had known Reid for years. She'd met him two

days after meeting Cal. She liked to joke that it had been love at first sight with the latter and best friends at first sight with the former.

"You'll never guess what I did.today," she said.

Reid raised his dark eyebrows. "Darlin', the way you've been surprising me lately, I wouldn't even try."

"I had lunch with your brother."

Reid leaned back in his chair. "I know you mean Cal because Walker is still stationed overseas. Okay, I'll bite. Why?"

"He offered me a job. He wants me to be the executive chef at the Waterfront."

"Huh."

Reid might be a part of the family but until he'd blown out his shoulder in the bottom of the third late last June, he'd never been involved in the business.

"That's the fish place, right?" he asked.

She laughed. "Yeah. And Buchanan's is the steak house, and you're running the sports bar, and Dani takes care of Hamburger Heaven. Jeez, Reid, this is your heritage. You have a family empire going here."

"No. What I have is a two-for-one appetizer special during happy hour. You gonna take the job?"

"I think so." She leaned forward. "He's paying me an outrageous salary and I get a percentage of the profits. It's what I've been waiting for. In three years I'll have enough money to open my own place."

He narrowed his gaze. "I told you I'd give you that money. Just tell me how much and I'll write you a check."

She knew he could. Reid had millions invested in all kinds of businesses. But she wouldn't take a loan from a friend. It was too much like being bailed out by her parents.

"I need to do this on my own," she said. "You know that."

"Yeah, yeah. You might want to think about getting that chip off your shoulder, Penny. It's making you walk funny."

She ignored that. "I like the idea of bringing back the Waterfront from the dead. I'll become even more of a star, which will make my restaurant even more successful."

"Not that you're letting all this go to your head."

She laughed. "Look at who's talking. Your ego barely fits inside an airplane hangar."

Reid walked around the desk and crouched next to her. He cupped her face in his hands and kissed her cheek. "If this is what you want, you know I'm there for you."

"Thanks." She brushed his dark hair off his forehead and knew that in many ways life would have been a lot simpler if she just could have fallen in love with Reid instead of Cal.

He stood and leaned against the desk. "When do you start?"

"As soon as the paperwork is signed. I've heard the old place needs a total renovation, but we don't have time for that. We're going to have to make do. I need to put together menus, hire a kitchen staff."

Reid folded his arms over his chest. "You didn't tell him, did you?"

She squirmed in her seat. "It's not important information."

"Sure it is." His gaze narrowed. "Let me guess. You

figured he wouldn't hire you if he knew, but once you're in place, he can't fire you for it."

"Pretty much."

"Slick, Penny. But it's not like you to play games."

"I want the job. It was the only way to get it."

"He's not going to like it."

She rose. "I don't see why it matters one way or the other. Cal and I have been divorced nearly three years. Now we're going to work together. It's a very new-millennium relationship."

Reid looked at her. "Trust me, when my brother finds out you're pregnant, there's going to be hell to pay and for more reasons than you know."

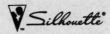

SPECIAL EDITION™

presents a new continuity

FAMILY BUSINESS

Bound by fate, members of a shattered family
renew their ties—and find a legacy of love.

On sale January 2006

PRODIGAL SON

by award-winning author

Susan Mallery

After his father's death, eldest son Jack Hanson
reluctantly assumed responsibility for the family
media business. But when the company faced
dire straits, Jack was forced to depend on
himself—and the skills of the one woman he
promised long ago he'd never fall for....

Don't miss this compelling story—only from
Silhouette Books.

Available at your favorite retail outlet.

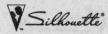

SPECIAL EDITION™

Divorce was tough enough on
Shawn Fletcher—selling the house and
watching her ex remarry really stung.
So a flirtation with her daughter's math
teacher, Matt McFarland, was a nice
surprise. But how would her daughter—
and the Callie's Corner Café gang—
take the news?

Look for

A PERFECT LIFE
by Patricia Kay

available January 2006

Coming soon from
CALLIE'S CORNER CAFÉ

IT RUNS IN THE FAMILY—February 2006
SHE'S THE ONE—March 2006

Where love comes alive™

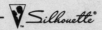

SPECIAL EDITION™

Here comes the bride...
matchmaking down the aisle!

HIS MOTHER'S WEDDING
by **Judy Duarte**

When private investigator Rico Garcia
arrived to visit his recently engaged
mother, the last thing on his mind was
becoming involved with her
wedding planner.

But his matchmaker of a mom
had other ideas!

Available January
wherever you buy books.

Where love comes alive™

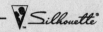

SPECIAL EDITION™

The second story in
The Moorehouse Legacy!

HIS COMFORT AND JOY
by Jessica Bird
January 2006

Sweet, small-town Joy Moorehouse knew
getting tangled up in fantasies about political
powerhouse Gray Bennett was ridiculous.

Until he noticed her...really noticed her.

Alex Moorehouse's story will be
available April 2006.

4 1/2 Stars, Top Pick!
"A romance of rare depth,
humor and sensuality."
—*Romantic Times* BOOKclub on
Beauty and the Black Sheep

If you enjoyed what you just read,
then we've got an offer you can't resist!

Take 2 bestselling love stories FREE!

Plus get a FREE surprise gift!

Clip this page and mail it to Silhouette Reader Service™

IN U.S.A.	IN CANADA
3010 Walden Ave.	P.O. Box 609
P.O. Box 1867	Fort Erie, Ontario
Buffalo, N.Y. 14240-1867	L2A 5X3

YES! Please send me 2 free Silhouette Special Edition® novels and my free surprise gift. After receiving them, if I don't wish to receive anymore, I can return the shipping statement marked cancel. If I don't cancel, I will receive 6 brand-new novels every month, before they're available in stores! In the U.S.A., bill me at the bargain price of $4.24 plus 25¢ shipping and handling per book and applicable sales tax, if any*. In Canada, bill me at the bargain price of $4.99 plus 25¢ shipping and handling per book and applicable taxes**. That's the complete price and a savings of at least 10% off the cover prices—what a great deal! I understand that accepting the 2 free books and gift places me under no obligation ever to buy any books. I can always return a shipment and cancel at any time. Even if I never buy another book from Silhouette, the 2 free books and gift are mine to keep forever.

235 SDN DZ9D
335 SDN DZ9E

Name	(PLEASE PRINT)	
Address	Apt.#	
City	State/Prov.	Zip/Postal Code

Not valid to current Silhouette Special Edition® subscribers.

Want to try two free books from another series?
Call 1-800-873-8635 or visit www.morefreebooks.com.

* Terms and prices subject to change without notice. Sales tax applicable in N.Y.
** Canadian residents will be charged applicable provincial taxes and GST.
All orders subject to approval. Offer limited to one per household.
® are registered trademarks owned and used by the trademark owner or its licensee.

SPED04R   ©2004 Harlequin Enterprises Limited

Kate Austin makes
a captivating debut
in this luminous tale
of an unconventional
road trip…and one
woman's metamorphosis.

dragonflies AND dinosaurs

KATE AUSTIN

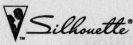

COMING NEXT MONTH

#1729 PRODIGAL SON—Susan Mallery
Family Business
After his father's death, it was up to eldest son Jack Hanson to save the troubled family business. Hiring his beautiful business school rival Samantha Edwards helped—her creative ideas worked wonders. But her unorthodox style rankled by-the-books Jack. They were headed for an office showdown...*and* falling for each other behind closed doors.

#1730 A PERFECT LIFE—Patricia Kay
Callie's Corner Café
The divorce was tough enough on Shawn Fletcher—selling the house and watching her ex remarry *really* stung. So a flirtation with her daughter's math teacher, Matt McFarland, came as a nice surprise. But when things with the younger man seemed serious, Shawn panicked—how would her daughter and the Callie's Corner Café gang take the news?

#1731 HIS MOTHER'S WEDDING—Judy Duarte
Private eye Rico Garcia blamed his cynicism about romance on his mom, who after four marriages had found a "soul mate"—again! Rico's help with the new wedding put him on a collision course with gorgeous, Pollyanna-ish wedding planner Molly Townsend. The attraction sizzled...but was it enough to melt the detective's world-weary veneer?

#1732 HIS COMFORT AND JOY—Jessica Bird
The Moorehouse Legacy
For dress designer Joy Moorehouse, July and August were the kindest months—when brash politico Gray Bennett summered in her hometown of Saranac. She innocently admired him from afar until things between them took a sudden turn. Soon work led Joy to Gray's Manhattan stomping ground...and passions escalated in a New York minute.

#1733 THE THREE-WAY MIRACLE—Karen Sandler
Devoted to managing the Rescued Hearts Riding School, Sara Rand kept men at arm's length, and volunteer building contractor Keith Delacroix was no exception. But then Sara and Keith had to join forces to find a missing student. Looking for the little girl made them reflect on loss and abuse in their pasts, and mutual attraction in the present....

#1734 THE DOCTOR'S SECRET CHILD—Kate Welsh
CEO Caroline Hopewell knew heartbreak. Her father had died, leaving her to raise his son by a second marriage, and the boy had a rare illness. Then Caroline discovered the truth: the child wasn't her father's. But the endearing attentions of the true dad, Dr. Trey Westerly, for his newfound child stirred Caroline's soul... giving her hope for the future.

SSECNM1205